"If someone gets too pushy or pers̶o̶n̶a̶l̶ for you, call me about that, too. Anything. I'm not taking any chances with our star witness."

So the warmth of his hand on her arm and the patient, adult conversation was about protecting the outcome of his task force investigation. "You're not taking any chances?"

"No."

With a wry smile, Bailey shook her head. Spencer Montgomery had KCPD running through his veins. Any shivers of awareness she might feel at his warm hands or masculine smells or polite attention were misguided responses to a man who was simply doing his job.

She was the surviving victim who could put away the Rose Red Rapist forever.

"I'll call," Bailey promised. "If I suspect anything's not right, I'll call."

"Don't go shopping by yourself. Make sure someone knows where you are at all times. You do whatever you have to to stay safe."

She'd had younger, more charming men hit on her with sweet words and shower her with gifts. But she'd never responded so easily, so basically, to any one of them the way she was reacting to Spencer Montgomery today.

"I'll try not to let you down, Mr. Montgomery."

"You won't."

You won't.

Did those last two words mean Detective Montgomery had faith in her ability to get the job done?

Or were they a warning that he intended to make sure she didn't screw this up?

YULETIDE PROTECTOR

USA TODAY Bestselling Author

JULIE MILLER

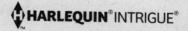

Recycling programs
for this product may
not exist in your area.

For Clarice Metz and Rhonda Glasford Metz, two of my Fulton fans. Mom loves it when you talk about my books with her. ;) Thanks for reading them!

ISBN-13: 978-0-373-74783-2

YULETIDE PROTECTOR

Copyright © 2013 by Julie Miller

All rights reserved. Except for use in any review, the reproduction or utilization of this work in whole or in part in any form by any electronic, mechanical or other means, now known or hereafter invented, including xerography, photocopying and recording, or in any information storage or retrieval system, is forbidden without the written permission of the publisher, Harlequin Enterprises Limited, 225 Duncan Mill Road, Don Mills, Ontario M3B 3K9, Canada.

This is a work of fiction. Names, characters, places and incidents are either the product of the author's imagination or are used fictitiously, and any resemblance to actual persons, living or dead, business establishments, events or locales is entirely coincidental.

This edition published by arrangement with Harlequin Books S.A.

For questions and comments about the quality of this book, please contact us at CustomerService@Harlequin.com.

® and TM are trademarks of Harlequin Enterprises Limited or its corporate affiliates. Trademarks indicated with ® are registered in the United States Patent and Trademark Office, the Canadian Trade Marks Office and in other countries.

Printed in U.S.A.

™ www.Harlequin.com

ABOUT THE AUTHOR

USA TODAY bestselling author Julie Miller attributes her passion for writing romance to all those books she read growing up. When shyness and asthma kept her from becoming the action-adventure heroine she longed to be, Julie created stories in her head to keep herself entertained. Encouragement from her family to write down the feelings and ideas she couldn't express became a love for the written word. She gets continued support from her fellow members of the Prairieland Romance Writers, where this teacher serves as the resident "grammar goddess." Inspired by the likes of Agatha Christie and Encyclopedia Brown, Julie believes the only thing better than a good mystery is a good romance.

Born and raised in Missouri, this award-winning author now lives in Nebraska with her husband, son and an assortment of spoiled pets. To contact Julie or to learn more about her books, write to P.O. Box 5162, Grand Island, NE 68802-5162 or check out her website and monthly newsletter at www.juliemiller.org.

Books by Julie Miller

HARLEQUIN INTRIGUE

CAST OF CHARACTERS

Spencer Montgomery—Leader of the KCPD task force, Spencer brought down the Rose Red Rapist. He's on the fast track to a stellar career and has put his personal life on hold. The last thing this stoic, seasoned detective wants to do is play bodyguard to the D.A.'s star witness on the case, even if he is attracted to her—because he knows firsthand the tragic results of mixing business with pleasure.

Bailey Austin—The last surviving victim of the Rose Red Rapist. The heiress's pampered life changed dramatically after the vicious assault. She's no longer certain of her friends, her future, or if she can ever love a man again. But she's determined to testify against her attacker—if she lives to see her day in court.

Brian Elliott—Is he really the Rose Red Rapist? He claims to be innocent.

Kenna Parker—Brian's defense attorney is the best that money can buy.

Vanessa Owen—How far will she go to get the story that will make her a superstar in the news world?

Regina Hollister—Brian's loyal assistant.

Corie Rudolf—Bailey's next-door neighbor is man-crazy.

Gabriel Knight—The reporter keeps showing up when you least expect him.

Mara Boyd-Elliott—She runs the *Kansas City Journal*. Why would she post the half-million-dollar bond for her ex?

The Cleaner—The Rose Red Rapist's mysterious accomplice. Has she gone underground to avoid capture? Or is she planning her most diabolical crime yet?

The Task Force—This dedicated group of crime fighters will see justice done—or die trying.

Prologue

"I'll save you," she whispered into the phone.

Brian Elliott looked at her through glass that separated them. The lines of strain around his blue eyes and handsome mouth were more pronounced. And the orange jumpsuit certainly didn't flatter.

After all she'd done for him, he still doubted her? "You don't think they're screening all my visitors? You're tempting fate by coming here."

If he wasn't looking so haggard, so in need of the comfort he normally sought from her, she would have been irritated by his doubt. Instead, she smoothed a smile on her face—for his benefit as well as the guards who might be watching. "It makes perfect, logical sense for me to come see you. Besides, you've had a lot of visitors, haven't you? Too many for the authorities to focus solely on me."

"You arranged all those visits?"

"Not many people can benefit from being associated with an alleged serial rapist." She'd gone to work as soon as she learned the news of his arrest. "Some of your friends and business associates probably are truly concerned for your welfare. And I might have suggested to some of them how staying in your good graces would prove most beneficial once you're acquitted."

He tipped his mouth closer to the phone that connected them and rubbed at his temple, as though the stress of the past couple of days had given him a headache. "How can you be sure that will happen? The police have eyewitness testimony. Experts from the crime lab to talk about trace evidence and DNA."

"The only thing their evidence proves is that you once fathered a child with a woman who's now in a mental institution. The D.A. will never put her on the stand to argue that it wasn't consensual sex. Everything else is circumstantial. A good lawyer will make that go away—and you've got the best attorney in town on your payroll. Any other charges are minor, and I expect you'll get probation and time served."

Her heart twisted with sympathy when he rubbed at the cuts and scratches on his forearm, painful wounds inflicted during his arrest just days earlier. "All it takes is one woman to stand up and identify me as the man who raped her."

"An eyewitness?" Despite his pain, she had to laugh. "How can any victim swear it was you? They were all unconscious, and you wore a mask."

"There's Hope Lockhart."

"You didn't rape her."

He cupped the receiver with his hand and revealed a hushed admission. "I wanted to. I wanted to hurt her so badly—"

"Shh." She leaned toward the glass and splayed her fingers there, wishing she could physically touch him and reassure him. "A jury can't convict you for being angry and having these revenge fantasies. But it won't help public perception if word gets out that you…enjoy the violence."

"I'm sitting in a jail cell. My bail hearing isn't until tomorrow. Public opinion doesn't matter in here."

"You talk as though you don't believe you're getting out."

She was pleased when he flattened his larger hand close to his side of the reinforced glass, touching her in the only way he could. For now. As long as he needed her, as long as he loved her, she'd find a way to make it work so they could both get what they wanted. "Do you really think we can fix this and make it go away?"

"Yes. But you have to trust me." She pulled her hand away, getting down to business. Brian had always appreciated her practical sense about how to get things done. It was one of the things that had drawn them together in the first place, even though the arguments often drove them apart. "I would have taken care of that issue with Miss Lockhart, too, if I had known how upset you were. If you had listened to me before, if you had let me handle the situation, you wouldn't be sitting where you are now."

"Let *you* handle it? I can't tolerate a betrayal like that. She needed to understand that I—"

"Hush." She quieted him before his agitation drew the guard's attention to their conversation. "Your emotions are your Achilles heel, Brian. I can think rationally, for the both of us. Let me do this for you. I've saved your gorgeous hide more than once. That was our agreement, remember? I take care of you.

I know you're sick. I can live with that. As long as you love me. But you have to trust—"

"Sick?" He shook his head and leaned back, the boardroom glare that had intimidated many an adversary directed squarely at her. "Trusting a woman is what got me into this mess in the first place."

She smiled. Poor thing. Didn't he know by now she couldn't be intimidated? "Trusting a woman is what will get you out of it, too."

She waited, displaying far more patience than he had ever shown her. At last, his broad shoulders lifted with a heavy breath and he nodded, accepting her promise. Accepting her.

"I love you." Pursing her lips together, she blew him a kiss. "Oh, and Brian, darling?" There were rules to this relationship, and he needed to understand them. "I'm willing to do whatever is necessary to save you. But if you betray who I am to anyone—a cell mate, a police officer or even a fly on the wall—I will destroy you." She smiled again. "Now, say you love me."

She held the defiant challenge in his dark eyes until, with a nod of understanding, he lowered his gaze. "I love you."

She hung up the phone and walked away.

Chapter One

December

"That's him. I recognize his voice. The build's right and the eyes are the same. He's the man who raped me."

Bailey Austin braced her hand against the chilly window that separated her from the suspect and decoys lined up in the adjoining room at KCPD's Fourth Precinct headquarters and closed her eyes. They all wore black clothes and surgical masks over the lower half of their faces. But she didn't need a visual to relive the sounds and smells and every violent, humiliating touch that had changed her life more than a year ago.

"Shut up!" A fist smashed across her cheekbone when she'd dared to beg him to stop. Pain pulsed through her fractured skull, swirling her plastic-covered surroundings into a dizzying vertigo that made her nau-

seous. Her stomach was already churning from the stingingly bitter smell of vinegar and soap on the washcloth he was bathing her with. As if he could simply wash away the pain and shock and violation of what he had done to her. Bound and battered, helpless to struggle against him, she tried to blank her mind against the unspeakable things he was doing to her. "I'm the one in charge here, you filthy thing," he needlessly reminded her.

Dark eyes swam in and out of focus from the grotesque black-and-white mask he wore. "Please..."

"Close your eyes and that mouth, or I'll put the hood on you again." She squeezed her eyes shut, dutifully doing what she could to save herself more punishment. "Do exactly what I tell you," he warned her, scrubbing away any evidentiary trace of himself or the crime scene from her body, "and maybe I'll let you live."

Bailey had been one of the lucky ones. She'd survived.

But she hadn't been able to erase the memory that night, and she couldn't now. Even with a simple recitation from a Kansas City travel brochure, she recognized his voice— so bitter and devoid of caring. "That's him," she repeated, opening her eyes to see a uniformed officer stop and cuff the black-haired man she'd identified. When he peeled off his mask, she recognized his face from the business and society pages of the Kansas City papers. "Brian Elliott is the man who... He's the Rose Red Rapist."

District Attorney Dwight Powers stood beside her at the one-way window. "You'll testify to that in court? You'll point him out to the jury?"

She swallowed the emotions that rose in her throat. Despite all logic that told her she was invisible to him here in the look-at room, Bailey hugged her orange wool coat tighter in her arms and backed away from the glass when her attacker turned and looked in her direction. She nodded, transfixed by the cruel eyes, warm with color and yet so cold. There was something wrong with that man, something sick or disconnected inside his head. A brilliantly successful businessman, charming on the surface, yet twisted, damaged, inside. And he'd taken all that rage, all that self-loathing out on her. As if she'd been the cause of his pain. Even through the glass she felt his hatred aimed squarely at her.

She could feel his hands on her all over again, her arms pinned above her head, his body on top of hers, and she shuddered.

"This is a dubious identification at best, Powers, and you know it." Shaking off the nightmare crawling over her skin, Bailey turned away from the glass as Kenna Parker, Brian Elliott's articulate defense attorney, started earning her expensive fee. The taller woman clutched her leather attaché in her fist and looked down with sympathy. "I'm sorry for what you've gone through, Miss Austin. But if the district attorney here puts you on the stand, I can promise you that my cross-examination won't be pleasant. If you're certain my client is your attacker, then why didn't you identify him sooner? He's a known figure in Kansas City society."

"I didn't know him. Not personally." Bailey's gaze darted up to meet the blond woman's faintly accusatory question. "I identified him by voice. And I did recognize his eyes as soon as I saw them again. Once he was arrested, I picked out his mug shot from a group of several suspects."

"You had a head injury, didn't you? Perhaps your memory isn't as clear as you'd like it to be."

Before Bailey could form the appropriate words to defend her competence as the prosecution's star witness, Harper Pierce, the family attorney her parents had insisted accompany them down to Precinct headquarters this morning, interrupted.

"Is that a threat, Kenna?" he challenged.

The woman smiled up at the attorney in the three-piece suit. "Of course not. I'm good enough I don't need to make threats." With a polite nod to everyone in the room, she turned on her Italian leather pumps and headed out the door. "Now if you'll excuse me, I need to go talk to my client. Chief Taylor?"

Mitch Taylor, the Precinct commander who blocked the door, folded his arms across his barrel-chest. "My people made a good arrest, Ms. Parker. They pulled a dangerous man off the streets."

"Did they?" She waited until he stepped aside to let her pass. "Or did they just find a convenient scapegoat so you could close your investigation and get the press off your back?"

Everyone in the tiny room turned their heads at the onslaught of voices and bright lights that greeted the lady attorney as soon as she stepped into the hallway. Reporters.

"Ms. Parker. Is your client a free man?"

"Will he still be out on bail?"

"Did the witness identify him as the Rose Red Rapist?"

"Who is the witness?"

Bailey clutched her stomach as a wave of nausea churned inside her. They were closing in like vultures. "Oh, my."

Dwight Powers braced his hand beneath her elbow. "Mitch," he warned.

"I'm on it." With a curt nod, Mitch stepped into the hallway. With a booming voice that made Bailey tremble, he took charge of the surging crowd. "This is a police station, not gossip central. Kate Kilpatrick, our task force liaison to the press, will answer your questions downstairs."

"Is that Brian Elliot?" a woman asked. "Could we talk to him?"

"My client is being released on bail, and we'll be making a formal statement later," Kenna promised.

"Joe! Sarge!" Bailey ducked behind the D.A.'s broad back as Chief Taylor called for backup. "Get them out of here. I'm not putting on a press conference for that scum. The reporters can talk to Elliott outside, once we get his ankle bracelet back on him."

"Yes, sir." A dutiful voice from the hallway hastened to do his chief's bidding. "Ms. Owen. Mr. Knight. This way, people. I'll escort you down to the front door."

As soon as Chief Taylor closed the door behind him, Bailey's mother, Loretta Austin-

Mayweather, spoke from the back of the room. "I don't like that woman. Do you think Kenna Parker staged that harangue of reporters to frighten Bailey?"

With the reporters' protesting voices reduced to a murmur, the D.A. released his grip on Bailey. "It's a possibility. She'll use every weapon in her arsenal to prove reasonable doubt to the jury. And since a lot of our case rests on your daughter…"

Bailey's chin popped up when he turned his eyes on her. Forcing herself to take easy, calming breaths, Bailey nodded. She had to do this. "Don't worry, Mr. Powers. You can count on me."

Loretta glanced up at the distinguished gentleman standing beside her. Her beautiful features were drawn with worry and fatigue. "Jackson, isn't there something you can do about Ms. Parker to protect Bailey? I've already lost Kyle. I don't think I could stand to see another child get hurt."

Too late for that, Bailey thought as a less-than-kind impulse bubbled up. But her sarcasm quickly turned to sympathy. They'd all been devastated by Kyle's death, her mother to the point that when Bailey had needed her most, Loretta had been incapable of empathizing with her daughter's pain. Her mother had lost weight from the stress and turned to a nightly glass or two of wine in order to sleep. For months now, Loretta had deflected any conversation more serious than the weather or the family's social calendar.

They all had their ways of coping. Bailey just hoped her efforts to take charge of her own life and to confront her attacker would lead to her own healing.

"We won't let that happen," Harper Pierce assured Loretta. "Will we." Bailey had to look away from the solicitous expression on the attorney's handsome face.

He used to look at her that way—before the assault, when they'd been engaged to be married—when she'd been able to tolerate a flirtatious wink or intimate touch, when she would have been satisfied to become his trophy wife and take her place at his side in Kansas City society. Once, that look would have bolstered her courage. Now, that sly wink was just something else she had to deal with.

"You can't talk me out of this, Harper," Bailey stated firmly. She was no longer the wide-eyed Pollyanna who'd doted on his needs and shared so many interests with him. Understandably, she had to put herself— and now her mother—first. She crossed the room to give her mother a gentle hug, then pulled away, smiling into the blue eyes that matched her own. "But I promise I'll be as careful as I can, Mother. Mr. Powers has assured my anonymity for as long as possible. And you know my counseling sessions with Dr. Kilpatrick have included lots of advice on ways a woman can keep herself safe. I've been listening. I won't take any unnecessary chances."

"I wish you hadn't cut your hair, dear." Without even acknowledging her daughter's attempt to reassure her, Loretta reached up to smooth Bailey's bangs back into the short wisps at her temple. "Those long, blonde waves were so beautiful."

Yes, but the short haircut was all about being safe, not making the pages of a fashion magazine. Having a man grab her by the hair and sling her to the floor or into the back of a van had a tendency to make a woman want to remove any "handles" that made it easy for an attacker to latch on. "Mother—"

"Jackson?" Loretta clung to her husband's arm, turning to Bailey's stepfather for the answers she wanted. "Can't you make this whole mess go away?"

Bailey's stepfather wasn't oblivious to the emotional undercurrents in the room. But his typical response was to try to fix whatever the problem might be. He slid a supportive arm around his wife's waist. "I'll do whatever's necessary to protect this family, dear." He turned to the D.A. "Do you think Ms. Parker will bring that ugly business with my stepson into the trial?"

"I had nothing to do with that," Bailey protested. She wasn't sure when or where her brother had gotten so caught up with greed that his reckless business dealings had made him desperate enough to kidnap and attempt to murder their half sister, Charlotte. But she knew the devious, violent man who'd been arrested, and subsequently murdered in prison, had no resemblance to the brother she'd once loved and admired. A different sort of character ran through her veins. Something smarter. Stronger. She hoped. "What Kyle did has nothing to do with what happened to me."

But Jackson was looking to the men in the room for a solution, not her. The D.A. understood his concern. "It's possible she could bring your family history into the courtroom, use it to taint the veracity of Bailey's testimony. If there's one liar in the family, why not two? I'd argue irrelevancy, of course."

"I'm not lying," Bailey insisted. "And my head wasn't so scrambled that I've forgotten what I heard and saw and went through that night."

The burly D.A. nodded. "I'm counting on it. The KCPD task force has given me plenty of forensic and circumstantial evidence to make a case. But science and legal jargon can overwhelm a jury. I need you to be the face of all his victims. The jury will sympathize with you and with your eyewitness testimony. They'll convict him, and the judge will put Elliott away for the rest of his life. Kenna Parker, however, is going to do everything she can to discredit you on the witness stand."

Chief Taylor, who put together the task force that had finally brought in the Rose Red Rapist, muttered a choice word beneath his breath. "Leave it to Elliott to buy the best. Parker's already got him out on bail. From what I hear, he got his ex-wife, Mara Boyd-Elliott who runs the *Journal*, to post it."

"Sounds like Elliott's got all kinds of friends we'll be up against."

Chief Taylor agreed. "I have somebody watching him around the clock, but he's running his business and buying Christmas presents, acting like he's facing traffic court instead of twenty or more years in prison. Kenna's only been in Kansas City for a year, and she's already earned a cutthroat reputation by winning cases." The senior cop pointed a warning finger at the D.A. "My task force worked for more than a year putting this case together and finally bringing him in. It'll demoralize my team, if not this entire city, if Elliott wins in court. Can you beat her, Dwight?"

"I win cases, too. Against tougher odds than this." To his credit, Dwight Powers didn't seem the least bit intimidated by either the reputation of his opposing counsel, pressure from the police department, or the wealth and influence Jackson Mayweather commanded.

Top attorneys. Top cop. Top society movers and shakers. Ex-fiancé. A nervous city. Her own fragile sense of confidence. They were all formidable opponents to stand up against in order to make herself heard. But Bailey finally shut down the memories and fear, and hastened to reassure Dwight Powers that he could rely on her to help send Brian Elliott to prison. "I can talk about the rose he left with me, the van he transported me in, how he dumped me in that alley, and what happened during the assault. Once I came to in that horrible room, I remember everything. He bathed me afterward and *disinfected* me with vinegar." She ignored her mother's pained gasp. "I'm not confused about any of it."

The burly D.A. pulled a pen from his suit jacket and jotted a note onto the yellow legal pad he held. "You'll confirm the surgical mask and stocking cap he wore, as well as a description of the construction site where he took you?"

Bailey nodded. She could do this. She *had* to stand up and face her attacker in the courtroom or she'd never be able to stand up for herself and feel any sense of strength or self-worth again. "I'll tell everything."

"Oh, sweetie. Surely not everything." Loretta crossed the room to squeeze her daughter's hand. "You were always such a sensitive child. And after this nightmare—"

"Mother." Just because she'd never been called on to deal with something like this before didn't mean she couldn't. Bailey pulled her hand away. "I'm twenty-six years old, not a child. I can do this. I need your support, not a lecture to talk me out of doing it." She thumbed over her shoulder toward the empty lineup room. "If I don't stand up against that man now, then I'll be his victim all over again—and for the rest of my life." Her hand turned into a fist as angry tears stung her eyes. "And he doesn't get to win."

Jackson came up beside Loretta, draping an arm around her as he squeezed Bailey's shoulder. "We understand that this is part of your recovery, dear. But one of the hardest things in the world is for a parent to see her child suffer. Be patient with us. We'll support whatever you decide. Just know we love you and that we'll be here for you."

As the tears welled up in her mother's eyes, Bailey sniffed back her own. She nodded her thanks and turned to Dwight. "Anything you ask," she vowed. "Anything Ms. Parker asks, I'll answer it. It can't be any harder than knowing he could go free to do the same thing to another woman. I want to feel safe again. I want him rotting in prison."

With a curt nod, Dwight packed his briefcase. "So do I." He latched it shut before shaking Bailey's hand. "I'll see you Monday morning at the courthouse when the trial begins, then. With your testimony, I'll have a guilty verdict by Christmas. And Brian Elliott will never celebrate another New Year's with his family and friends. Chief Taylor?"

"Thank you, Miss Austin, for being so courageous." The police chief shook her hand, too, before reaching behind him to open the door. "I've got a roll-call meeting to get to. I'll have an officer walk you out."

"I've got it, sir." A tall detective with crisp, golden-red hair straightened from the wall across the hallway where he'd been leaning. Without a wasted motion, he buttoned the front of his steel-gray suit jacket over the badge and gun belted at his trim waist. "Miss Austin."

Bailey halted in the doorway as her eyes locked on to Spencer Montgomery's cool granite gaze. He was a decade her senior, with nothing boyish about him to soften his chiseled, unreadable face. He was an old family foe who'd investigated her brother's illegal activities—meaning that most of their past conversations had put one or the other of them on the defensive, as he grilled her with questions or she did what she could to protect her family. But, as leader of the KCPD task force, he'd turned those same dogged, calculating investigative skills to solving the string of crimes committed by the Rose Red Rapist. That made him the one man most responsible for Brian Elliott's arrest. And for that, he would always be her hero.

Still, Spencer Montgomery was probably here to make sure she hadn't made a mistake in identifying his suspect, that she hadn't screwed up his year-long investigation. Despite an innate appreciation for his mature intelligence and faintly military bearing, Bailey's pulse rate went on wary alert. "Detective Montgomery."

"If you have a moment, I'd like to talk to you."

Judging by the grim line of his mouth, she had a feeling she wasn't going to like whatever he had to say.

Chapter Two

She'd cut her hair.

Spencer noted the change in Bailey Austin's appearance—noted that the short, sun-kissed waves made her look a lot more grown-up than he remembered. She'd always been pretty, but the changes he noticed today made her...interesting. But just as quickly as he decided he liked the new look, he dismissed the revelation.

Any latent attraction he had to the woman was irrelevant. The last time he'd seen Bailey, she'd been in a hospital bed, beaten within an inch of her life—the victim of a violent rape by the man his task force had eventually identified and arrested, entrepreneur and real estate developer Brian Elliott. He should be content to see the bruises gone and the vibrancy back in her azure-blue eyes instead of noticing the leaner curves beneath the wool slacks and cashmere sweater she wore and the way those sculpted wisps of hair gleamed like spun gold, even under the fluorescent lights of the precinct hallway.

No, he couldn't notice those things at all. He was here to do his job. Period. And if that job included babysitting a fragile debutante-in-distress from Kansas City society, then so be it.

Besides, Chief Taylor was clapping him on the shoulder, demanding his attention. "You're going to see this job through to the bitter end, aren't you, Spence."

"Yes, sir."

"I knew there was a reason I made you point man on the task force." Mitch Taylor might be graying at the temples, but the man was still the powerhouse of the Fourth Precinct. He was the boss whose recommendation could make or break a promotion. Spencer respected the dedicated cop who'd worked his way up the ranks at KCPD. And since his goal was to do the same, getting asked to do a favor for the boss was an opportunity he didn't intend to squander.

"I appreciate the faith you had in us, sir."

"Your work isn't done yet," the chief reminded him, referring either to the outcome of Brian Elliott's trial or the task force's ongoing search for the Rose Red Rapist's accomplice—a woman they'd dubbed The Cleaner because of her efforts to destroy evidence and take out witnesses to Elliott's crimes. "You remember our chat yesterday?"

I want you to check in on Miss Austin from time to time. Make yourself available to her in case anything comes up that could spook her out of testifying against Elliott.

"I do."

Spencer had walked out of Chief Taylor's office understanding his mission. The Cleaner hadn't shown up on their radar since they'd made the arrest and the rapes had stopped. But then Elliott had been under KCPD's watch 24/7 from the moment his ex-wife had posted bail. Their vigilance might have driven the accomplice underground or out of town—or maybe whatever sick relationship the woman shared with a serial rapist had failed now that he was no longer able to commit the crimes that had terrorized Kansas City for several years. Or, as both Mitch Taylor and Spencer suspected, the woman could be biding her time, waiting to make some big move to *save her man* again.

Until The Cleaner was identified and put out of commission, Spencer intended to keep his task force on full alert. Scoring a few points with the boss along the way couldn't hurt, either.

The chief gestured to the group filing out of the look-at room behind Bailey. "I take it you know everyone here?"

Spencer nodded. While he couldn't claim to be friends with anyone in Bailey's entourage, they were certainly well acquainted. "We've met several times. On this investigation and the Rich Girl Killer case."

"You closed that one for me, too." Mitch Taylor praised him before winking a brown eye at Bailey. "I leave you in good hands, Miss Austin." The chief turned and hurried down the hallway after D.A. Powers. "Dwight, wait up."

While Bailey hugged her purse and coat to her waist, waiting expectantly for him to explain why Chief Taylor had asked him to chat with her, a protective force of allies circled behind her.

Loretta Austin-Mayweather's disgusted snort was audible, her blue eyes unforgiving. "Jackson, please. I'd like to go home. I have nothing to say to this man. Bailey, come."

Yes, he'd brought the Rich Girl Killer murder investigation to their home, and had been obligated to interrogate each and every one of them. And though Bailey's brother, Kyle

Austin, hadn't ultimately been the murderer Spencer had sought, he *had* been guilty of other crimes, including embezzlement, stalking his own stepsister and kidnapping. And the real killer, who hadn't appreciated a copycat using his M.O., had ultimately murdered the Austin heir while he'd been in prison.

Since Spencer had no children—no family at all, to speak of—he supposed he couldn't truly understand a parent's loss of a child. He could only play whipping boy and hold back the reminder that without KCPD's intervention, the entire Mayweather family might have fallen victim to Kyle Austin's desperate actions and the killer who'd threatened them.

"Detective." Jackson Mayweather's acknowledgment was more civil, but clearly the man had a meeting to get to, or an eagerness to defuse his wife's displeasure, because he looped his arm around Loretta's shoulder and started down the hallway. "Come along, dear. I'll have the driver meet us at the front door."

"Bailey." Loretta practically clicked her tongue, calling her daughter to join them.

Despite a deep sigh that indicated she was schooling her patience, Bailey simply smiled and turned her head. "Detective Montgomery is the leader of the Rose Red Rapist investigation. He probably needs to discuss something with me."

Harper Pierce, a tall, blond piece-of-work who'd stonewalled more than one KCPD investigation with his legal acrobatics, placed his hand at the small of Bailey's back. "Then he can make an appointment. Let's go."

Before Spencer could evaluate the way his own body braced at the proprietary touch, Bailey arched her back away from the other man's hand and sent Pierce on his way. "Would you mind looking after Jackson and Mother? I know she'd appreciate the extra arm to lean on."

"I'm not leaving you with—"

"Please, Harper. Go." Her melodic voice lost its sweet tone and her body seemed to hug itself around the orange coat she clutched. So she didn't like to be touched? Was that an aftereffect of the rape? Or was it that she just didn't want her ex-fiancé putting his hands on her?

Flashing a suspicious eye toward Spencer, as if *he* was somehow to blame for the dismissal, Harper relented. "I'll hold the elevator for you."

"That won't be necessary."

"Bails—"

"I'll walk her to her car," Spencer volunteered, eager to send the others on their way. That'd give him a few minutes of private time with Bailey to have the conversation Chief Taylor wanted him to have with her. Then he could get back to some real work.

"How did you know I drove myself?" Bailey arched a golden eyebrow as she turned her attention back to him.

Spencer dropped his gaze down to the keys dangling from her fist and grinned. Easy deduction. "I *am* a detective."

A responding grin eased the strain on her mouth and relaxed some of the tension from her posture. "So you are." The gentleness returned to her voice as she spoke to her parents and ex-fiancé again. "You all go ahead. I need to get back to my apartment and organize my portfolio for the job interview I have tomorrow, anyway. It'll save you a stop."

"Can't you put that off until another day?" Loretta sounded more irritated than hurt by her daughter's excuse to leave them. "The Butler-Smythes are coming to dinner tonight, remember? Their son Cameron is just home from his trip to China. You know he was sweet on you back in school, and I thought—"

"I can't, Mother." A rosy hue tinted Bailey's cheeks, indicating the level of impatience or distress she was keeping in check at her mother's efforts to plan her evening and her life. "I have errands to run before I go home. And I'm still fixing up my apartment. I want to finish painting the trim around the windows tonight." Spencer would have stopped with a solid *no,* but Bailey threw in a bit of logic to salvage her mother's feelings. "Besides, you know I'm not feeling terribly social right now. If you want me to make an appearance at your holiday gala this weekend, I need to save up my social energy to face all those people. Deal?"

Loretta's dramatic sigh indicated her daughter had finally come up with an excuse she could accept. "I suppose it's a fair tradeoff. I do want you at the Christmas ball. I can guarantee yeses to every invitation if our guests know you'll be there."

Spencer felt himself bristling on Bailey's behalf. The young woman was gearing up to testify against her rapist—to face the man who'd nearly killed her—across the short distance of a courtroom. And her mother was worried about matchmaking and society fund-raisers?

Although the tension crept back into her posture, Bailey continued to smile when her mother came to give her a hug. "Please give

Cam and his parents my regards, but I won't be there."

Loretta's cutting gaze swept over Spencer as she pulled away. Then she brushed Bailey's bangs off her forehead and straightened the angel pendant hanging around her neck. "Very well then. I'll call you tomorrow about the Christmas Ball."

Bailey nodded. "I'll talk to you then."

"Call me if you need an escort to the ball." Bailey stiffened when Harper leaned in to press a kiss to her temple and Spencer felt a protective urge make him stand straighter. And even though she managed a smile before Pierce followed Loretta and Jackson Mayweather down the hallway, it didn't last.

"I apologize for my family and..." she thumbed over her shoulder "...my attorney."

"They're understandably protective of you."

"Smothering is more like it." She unfolded the coat she carried and flipped it around her shoulders. "Happy holidays, Detective. I hope you're well."

"What?"

Her mouth relaxed with a soft giggle, probably at catching him off guard with the friendly chitchat. "It's customary when someone issues you a greeting like that for you say something similar in return."

"Oh. Right." When she juggled her keys and purse to shrug into her coat, Spencer decided to test his no-touch theory. He pointed, alerting her to his intent before moving behind her to hold her coat. She paused for a moment before thanking him and sliding her arms into the sleeves. After settling the collar up around her neck, he smoothed his hands across her shoulders and patted her arms. It was Pierce's touch she hadn't liked. Or maybe being touched without being asked first. She wasn't skittish with him standing behind her. She hadn't frozen up. Maybe she was going to make a calmer, more reliable witness than Chief Taylor thought. "Happy holidays, Bailey."

What the heck? Spencer popped his grip open and stepped back when he realized he was still holding her shoulders, still breathing in the faint citrusy scent of her hair, still feeling her warmth.

And did she just shiver when he pulled away? Was that a soft gasp he heard? She'd liked his touch. Or, at the very least, she hadn't minded his hands lingering on her.

There were times when possessing his finely honed eye for detail sucked. *Think job, Montgomery. Forget the woman. Forget the attraction.*

You know what hell that will lead you to.

"How are you holding up?" he asked, his tone more brusque than he'd intended.

"Are you worried I'm going to screw up all your hard work?" Bailey slipped her purse onto her shoulder, inhaling a deep breath before turning to face him. They stood close enough now that she had to tilt her face up to see his. Good grief, her eyes were blue.

A pair of pretty brown eyes, buried deep within his memory, suddenly surfaced in his mind, blurring his vision. Spencer blinked away the vision before the pain could follow. He slipped his hands into the pockets of his slacks and strolled a few steps toward the main room at the end of the hall, pretending he was still on his game. "Chief Taylor wanted me to run through some safety precautions with you—make sure you're all ready to go for Monday, or whenever you get called to the stand."

"So you *are* worried. You don't think I'll go through with this, either, do you?"

The accusation stopped him in his tracks and Spencer turned. "This is an important case, Bailey."

"It's important to me, too." She shoved her keys into her pocket and faced off against him. "Everyone thinks I'm going to freak out on the stand or run away and hide somewhere. But I have to do this. There has to be a reason why this happened to me."

Spencer's eyes narrowed at the emotion staining her cheeks. If she got worked up arguing with him, how was she going to handle it if Kenna Parker tried to rattle her on the witness stand? "That's a lot of pressure to put on yourself."

"Yes. But I can handle it."

He pulled his hand from his pocket and tapped the fingers fisted around the strap of her purse, silently arguing her cool-under-fire argument. "Have you ever done anything like this before? Have you ever bared your fears and soul and worst nightmare in front of the man who made you afraid?"

"No. Of course not, but…"

He let the reality of what they were asking of her set in, and watched her cheeks pale and her gaze drop to the center of his chest. "This is going to get messy before it gets done. Are you sure you're up for this?"

"You'd think I'd have at least one person cheering me on and bucking up my confidence instead of telling me all the reasons why I can't or shouldn't do it." She tilted her chin up, venting a mixture of temper and frustration. "Since you've been so obsessed with catching this guy, I would have thought you'd be in my corner. But you're as much of a doubting Thomas as anybody else."

"I'm not the kind of man to give pep talks, Bailey." As Bailey's voice grew louder and more animated, Spencer's hushed, articulating every word as he dipped his head closer to hers. "There's a lot that can happen between now and when you're called up to that witness stand. Besides you 'freaking out' and deciding not to testify, there's a possibility Brian Elliott's accomplice may do something to try to stop you."

"You're talking about The Cleaner, aren't you?"

"Yes, I'm talking about The Cleaner—and she's nobody you want to mess with. You need to lock your doors and windows. Don't go out by yourself at night. Have someone walk you to your car. Hang with people you know and trust. And if something does happen, call me or 911 before it's too late to do anything about it."

With every sentence, her eyes widened and her skin cooled to a pale porcelain color. "Too late…?"

"I'm not here to sugarcoat anything. I'm just stating the facts."

After an endless moment of silence she

tore her gaze from his and focused her attention on buttoning her coat. "Don't worry, detective. No one would ever mistake you for a warm and fuzzy kind of guy." She tied her orange belt with equal fervor. "Now, was that the lecture you were supposed to give me? Watch my back and don't be stupid? Or do you have some more doom and gloom you'd like to share? Let's get it over with because I really do need to get home and hide away in my little ivory tower of naïveté and incompetence."

"I didn't call you stupid."

"No, you're just intimating that I can't take care of myself."

Really? This defiant little show of sarcasm was supposed to convince him to trust her to close his case? Was this an attempt to show her strength? By butting heads with him? And since when did he get in anyone's face and argue back?

Spencer's blood was still pumping hard through his veins when he heard a door open in the hallway behind him. He saw the shock register on Bailey's face and instinctively went on guard against the unseen threat as he spun around.

Two uniformed officers led Brian Elliott out of the nearby interview room. He'd changed into an expensively tailored suit and a smug untouchability that made him look more like a Forbes 500 mogul than the prisoner wearing a pair of handcuffs and ankle-band tracking device he truly was. An entourage of his attorney, Kenna Parker, and Elliott's ex-wife, Mara Boyd-Elliott, followed behind. One a dark blonde, the other, platinum, both women wore business suits and carried winter coats and attaché cases, looking like they'd all just finished a business meeting instead of a legal debriefing.

Spencer's arm went out to push Bailey behind him as the group came closer. He felt her fingers curling into the back of his jacket and something inside him shifted, grew wary. When Elliott spotted Spencer, the bastard grinned in recognition. The other man slowed his stride and the soft gasp at Spencer's back made him reach down to fold his hand around Bailey's wrist beside him.

"Keep walking, Elliott," Spencer ordered.

"Now, now, detective. I've missed our little chats in the interrogation room" the man taunted. "Arrest any other innocent people lately?"

"Brian." That was the ex, laying a hand on his shoulder. "Don't make me regret my investment. I'm willing to support you to a point, but antagonizing the police won't help your case."

Elliott shrugged off her touch. "You only posted bail so your paper could report on the trial without it looking like a personal vendetta against me."

Mara eased a calming sigh behind his back. "Unbiased reporting isn't the only reason. There's still a place in my heart for you. And I believe in...your innocence."

Innocence? The newspaper publisher could barely choke out the word. Spencer wondered how the woman could live with herself, putting Elliott out on the street just so she could sell more papers.

Did he need to remind them about blood matching Elliott's type being found at the scene of one of the assaults? Had they forgotten his DNA matching the child of a woman who claimed to have been raped by the Rose Red Rapist? Did any of them think Elliott could deny kidnapping a woman and being captured by the K-9 cop and his German Shepherd partner on Spencer's task force?

Spencer could easily imagine the arguments Elliott's attorney would bring up. The blood sample had been corrupted and could match any number of suspects. The child's birth mother, who'd never reported being raped, had had a nervous breakdown and been committed to a mental hospital, so her version of events was suspect. The abduction could be pled down to a lesser crime and argued that it was a solo occurrence, not the culmination of a reign of serial terror through the city.

But there was no arguing away the eyewitness testimony of the courageous woman digging her fingers into his shoulder blade right now. Or Spencer's driving need to protect the truth she represented.

"Get him out of here, Ms. Parker." Spencer repeated the command to move the handcuffed man.

But when the uniformed guards urged the prisoner forward, Brian Elliott planted his feet and turned. "Wait. Do I know you, miss?"

Bailey released her death grip on Spencer's jacket and slid her right hand down his arm. At the brush of her chilled skin against his, he turned his palm into hers, lacing their fingers together, offering his protection and support against the man who'd terrorized her a year earlier. When she latched on to him with both hands, Spencer tightened his hold.

Be tough, Bailey, he wanted to say. He

could feel her trembling beside him. *Be just as strong as you claim to be.*

Kenna Parker nudged aside one of the uniformed officers and moved in front of her client. "You shouldn't have any contact with the opposing witnesses."

Damn straight.

But Elliott ignored his attorney's plea. "You're Jackson Mayweather's daughter, er, stepdaughter. I've had a few business dealings with Jackson, and I've given a lot of money to your mother's charities. She does good work for local hospitals and children's groups." He was making small talk with Bailey? Was he hoping she'd recant her statement because he knew her parents or could pour on the charm? "You're the woman who thinks I hurt you."

"Thinks?" The trembling stopped. Was some steel creeping into that delicate backbone of hers? Or was she on the verge of passing out?

"Brian," Kenna Parker warned. "Don't say another word."

Mara Elliott tried to get him moving, too. "Darling, we need to go."

"Don't *darling* me—!" The cuffs that linked Elliott's wrist jangled as he jerked against them.

Bailey's hand jerked in Spencer's grip. Good. Not passing out.

He snapped an order to the two unis. "Get him out of here."

The brief show of anger quickly passed, and, with the officers grabbing hold of Brian Elliott, the perp raised his hands in calm surrender. "I'm all right, dear," he apologized to his ex. "I've got this, Kenna." Then he turned his attention back to Spencer. "I'm sorry for what happened to your friend there. Yes, I've made some mistakes, but I'm not the monster you think I am. The man you want is still out there, Montgomery, lying in wait to hurt some other helpless woman." He gestured to the women there to support him, as if their presence was proof of his innocence. "I'm no serial rapist."

Maybe Spencer's command hadn't been clear. "Go. Now."

A brunette woman, wearing a coat over her suit, and holding a cell phone to her ear, came around the corner and stopped. Her dark eyes widened as she took in the confrontation in the hallway. "Mr. Elliott?" Regina Hollister, Brian Elliott's executive assistant, paused for a moment, then asked the party on her call to wait while she joined the group. "I have your car waiting for us out front. Is everything all right?"

"Get him out of here." Or Spencer would do the job himself.

The two officers pulled Elliott into step between them. Kenna Parker hurried ahead to consult with Elliott's assistant. "Out front where the reporters are?"

Regina nodded and put her cell phone back to her ear. "I'll ask the driver to meet us someplace else."

"No." Kenna stopped her and turned to face her client, walking backward as they continued down the hallway. "Let's use the press to our advantage. The officers will uncuff you before you leave the building. I don't want you to make any comment, but let's show Kansas City that you're a free man."

"For now," Spencer called after them. "Don't let that ankle bracelet pinch too tight, Elliott."

When Brian Elliott began a retort, Kenna Parker pressed her finger against his lips to shush him until he smiled and nodded his acquiescence. Spencer didn't move or look away until Brian Elliott and the others had turned the corner toward the bank of public elevators and disappeared from sight.

Easing out a tense breath as the threat left,

Spencer quickly became aware of other sorts of tension humming through his body. Bailey had her left hand curled around his arm now. Her whole body was hugged up against his side, seeking shelter or maybe just something stronger than she was to hold her upright. Several more seconds passed before Spencer acknowledged that he wasn't moving away from the warmth of her curves pressed against his arm. And that was his thumb stroking across the back of her knuckles, soothing the crushing grip of her hand.

It was happening again. This was getting personal. This was how it had started with Ellen, and he couldn't go through that again. *Move away, Montgomery.* Cop. Witness. Keep her safe. Don't let any feelings get involved with this.

"Do your job," he mouthed to himself.

"What?" Bailey whispered beside him.

Even worse than feeling the damn emotions was someone else knowing they were there, providing a weapon they could use against him.

So he emptied his lungs on a forceful breath of air and pulled his body away from Bailey's to face her. "You okay?" he asked.

"Yes." Her nod wasn't all that convincing. She squeezed her eyes shut for second and shook her head, as if clearing some graphic image from her mind. But when they opened again, that azure gaze tilted up and locked on to his. "I smelled that vile cologne he had on. I'm sure it's something expensive, but…" The strength of her gaze faltered. "He had it on that night, too. I *know* he's the man who raped me."

"I have no doubt," Spencer agreed. "That's exactly the kind of detail that will make the D.A.'s case for us." When the taut line of her mouth softened into a smile, he ignored that little kick of awareness that made him smile in return.

"Thank you for saying that. And thank you for being here when…" She visibly shuddered. "He was close enough he could have touched me."

"Brian Elliott will never touch you again." When he heard how vehemently he'd spoken those words, as if he'd just made some kind of promise to Bailey Austin, Spencer released her hand and broke contact entirely. It wasn't his job to care about the awful turmoil she must go through each time she had to revisit the violence that had been done to her. Maybe she was okay with being touched, or maybe she'd been too scared to realize how hard she'd been holding on to him. Either way was a head game he wasn't comfortable play-ing. She needed a sensitive kind of guy or her therapist to walk her through the emotional minefield of taking down the Rose Red Rap-ist. And he wasn't that guy.

He needed some distance. This situation was getting inside his head—the woman was getting under his skin. Setting up a safe house and guarding a witness weren't part of his job description anymore. He was *not* this wom-an's protector. He was seeing his investiga-tion through to the very end, like any good detective would. He was doing a favor for Chief Taylor.

He was *not* putting himself in a position to lose anyone else who mattered to him.

Ignoring the questioning look in Bailey's eyes, Spencer inclined his head toward the bullpen—the maze of desks and cubicles in the main room where he and dozens of other detectives worked. "Come on. Let me get my coat and then I'll walk you to your car." He moved out without a backward glance, lengthening his stride to put some impersonal space between them. "I'll give you my card and my partner's, and, of course, you can call the precinct if you need anything else."

Her heels clicked on the marble tiles be-hind him as she hurried to catch up.

All of Bailey's brave talk about testifying had flown out the window when she'd come face to face with Brian Elliott...right along with Spencer's resolve not to let things get personal with her.

He wouldn't let either one happen again.

Chapter Three

Starch.

That was the subtle, clean scent filling the elevator. Bailey clutched the strap of her purse to her stomach, almost smiling beside the jut of Spencer Montgomery's shoulder as he watched the third-level light come on above the doors of the parking garage elevator.

After traveling down through the bowels of the Fourth Precinct building and out a side entrance, they'd hurried through the bracing air and blowing snow to enter the parking garage a block away from the bright lights and electronic noise of the impromptu press conference on the front steps of the tall granite building across the street. The multistory parking garage might be filled with cars, but with the cold wind blowing through the open levels, chasing the patrons indoors, there'd been no one around when Spencer had bustled her onto the elevator and punched the button. This silent ride up the elevator gave Bailey a calming reprieve from the emotional battles she'd fought all morning with her family, Brian Elliott and within herself.

Not that she'd call her time spent with Spencer Montgomery relaxing, exactly.

Since his promise to walk her to her car, everything had been a rush. Papers neatly stacked on his desk. Chair pushed in. A quick introduction to his partner, Nick Fensom. She'd hurried to keep up with his long strides, been relegated to quick nods in response to his clipped requests and commands. The damp chill in the air outside had nipped at her ears and nose. But now that she had a few moments alone in the elevator with him to catch her breath and thaw out, she had the strangest urge to turn her nose into the nubby wool of his charcoal-gray coat.

Nothing more than starch and soap and cold, crisp air. Emanating from the charcoal-gray coat and crisp white shirt he wore, and maybe from the man himself, Spencer's scent was as straightforward and masculine as every other detail she'd noticed about the steely-eyed detective.

Unlike the overpowering smell of Brian Elliott's cologne that triggered nightmares,

Spencer's undoctored scent elicited something feminine and long forgotten inside her. Its simplicity soothed her overwrought senses, yet awakened warm frissons of awareness that she hadn't been sure she'd ever be able to feel again for a man. It was a gentler, although no less impactful response than what she'd felt outside the look-at room when she'd anchored herself to the unwavering strength of his hand holding hers. Spencer's unexpected touch had centered her, strengthened her, allowed her to push aside her gut reaction of panicked fear and handle Brian Elliott's attempt to strike up a conversation and deny what he'd done to her.

Yes, they'd argued. Yes, he'd pushed her to keep up with his long strides. Yes, it irritated her that Detective Montgomery pictured her as some sort of naive girl who couldn't think or do for herself, and had no idea what she was getting into. But it had felt invigorating for a few moments to have someone actually let her speak her mind and vent her emotions without trying to quickly apologize or change the subject. He hadn't slowed down and lowered his expectations because he thought she was too fragile to handle any kind of stress. And she definitely wasn't feeling anything girlish around the man.

Not when he smelled so good.

Not when he'd stood between her and her rapist.

Not when he made her feel, period.

After all this time, sheltered by her family, sheltered by the protective mental and emotional barriers she'd put up around herself since the rape, it was just as unsettling as it was intriguing to realize that the tall, no-nonsense detective could make her feel normal, womanly things again.

The elevator slowed; the signal dinged.

"Straight to your car, then straight home, right?"

Her secret grin faded at Spencer's brusque reminder. Clearly, whatever crush was forming inside her head wasn't mutual. She was just another piece of evidence in his case against the Rose Red Rapist he wanted to protect. She'd be wise to remember that, and keep the relationship between them as businesslike as he did. "Yes. I have plenty to do to keep me busy at my apartment tonight."

The doors slid open and he wound his hand around her upper arm like he had before, pulling her into step beside him as soon as she pointed out her white Lexus. "You'll check the parking lot before you get out of your car. Lock the—"

"—doors. Have my key card ready to go into the building. Check the doors and windows. Call someone to let them know I'm home."

"I see you were listening." For the first time in the last thirty minutes, Spencer shortened his stride to let her walk naturally beside him. Was that a grin?

Bailey wondered what would happen to that stern, angular face if he loosened up enough to smile or laugh. "After hearing the same speech upstairs at your office, on the hike across the street and in the elevator coming up here, I started to pick up on what you were trying to say."

That snort might be as close to a laugh as she was going to get out of him. And his warm breath formed a cloud in the cold air, masking a glimpse of what, if any, changes might have softened the strong line of his mouth or add warmth to the granite in his eyes.

But the grip on her arm eased as they crossed the concrete platform, heading toward the thick pillar where she'd parked. "Bailey, I don't think you're a dumb blonde. If anything, I think you're a courageous woman. You may have pushed a few of my buttons earlier and I said some things that didn't come out the way I meant them. I don't normally lose my cool like that."

Um, when exactly had he lost his cool? Brian Elliott's temper had flared briefly in that hallway, throwing Bailey back to that night when he'd ranted at her and punished her for daring to speak her mind or beg for mercy. If Spencer thought he'd come any-where close to a hotheaded reaction, he was apologizing for nothing. "You were just being a cop. You don't have to explain yourself."

"Yeah, I do. Logically, I think you feel you're doing the right thing—God knows I and half of Kansas City are glad you're tes-tifying. But I worry that you may not fully understand the dangers and challenges you'll have to face when this trial starts. Elliott won't be in handcuffs in that courtroom. And if The Cleaner shows up—"

Bailey pulled his business card from her pocket and waved it in front of his face. "Then I'll call you or your partner or 911."

Another deep breath obscured his reaction. But she might have glimpsed a wry smile. "I guess I need to stop warning you, hmm?"

"You mean treat me like a grown-up?"

"Message received. Got your keys out?"

Bailey swapped the card for the keys in her

pocket and pressed the remote, unlocking the car and starting the ignition. "Yes, sir."

"Bailey—" The grip on her arm suddenly tightened and Spencer pulled her to a stop. "Ah, hell."

A dark-haired woman climbed out of the car parked across from Bailey's. The spiky heels of her black leather boots didn't slow her at all as she crossed to the trunk of Bailey's car. The striking brunette pulled a microphone from the folds of her coat. "Are you the star witness Dwight Powers keeps bragging about?"

"Bragging?" Hadn't they escaped the onslaught of reporters?

A second door opened and the reporter waved her camera man forward. "I'm Vanessa Owen, Channel Ten News. Do you mind if I ask you a few questions, Miss Austin?"

Was the dark-haired woman giving her a choice? Vanessa was pushing for confirmation of her suspicions. But Bailey wasn't going to give her what she wanted. When the camera pointed her way and the light came on, nearly blinding her in the dimness of the garage, Bailey kept her expression placid despite the clench of her fist. "I'm *a* witness. I'm sure the D.A. is talking to as many of the Rose Red Rapist's victims that he can."

"Don't you mean alleged victims?" Vanessa Owen's dark gaze flitted over Bailey's shoulder to include Spencer in the interrogation. "Has he really been committing these crimes undetected for as many years as the D.A. claims?"

"Your questions are done, Ms. Owen." Spencer reached around Bailey to push the camera lens toward the ground and warn the camera man to kill the light and stop recording. In a subtle move that wasn't lost on either woman, he went into detective mode, sliding his shoulder in front of Bailey and blocking her from any attempt to question her again. Then *he* went on the offensive. "From what I hear, you and Brian Elliott have been pretty chummy. If you want to talk allegations, I have it on good intel that you and Elliott are having an affair."

"Past tense, Detective...Montgomery, is it? Leader of KCPD's illustrious task force? Brian and I may have attended a few social events together, but we're no longer an item. Get your facts straight." Vanessa's ruby-tinted lips widened into a smile that never reached her eyes. "That's all I'm trying to do."

But Spencer didn't back down from the taunt. "Either way, I'd think your viewers would be alarmed to learn just how biased your reporting on this case has been." If anything, he leaned in. "Or did you get involved with a rapist just to get the inside scoop on his crimes? If that's the case, I'd like to talk to you about withholding evidence from the police and abetting a suspected felon."

With an amused laugh, Vanessa waved her cameraman back to their car. "Nicely played, Detective. I get your message. I'll back off from Miss Austin. For now." She tilted her head to acknowledge Bailey with a nod, then took a step closer to Spencer. "But this is the biggest story to hit Kansas City in years. I have a feeling there's more to it than what KCPD or the D.A.'s office is sharing. And when her testimony becomes public record? Trust me, I'll get the story. And I'll take it all the way to the national market. Neither the D.A.'s stonewalling nor your task force are going to stop me from telling the biggest story of my career."

"Just make sure you tell the truth." Spencer turned his face to the side and Bailey gasped when she saw a black-haired man she hadn't noticed leaning against a concrete pillar. "That goes for you, too, Knight. Whatever gripe you've got against KCPD, you're not going to use Miss Austin to malign us in your editorials again."

The second reporter, who'd been jotting something on a notepad, straightened. "They're not editorials. They're facts." Even though his blue eyes were focused squarely on the detective, Bailey couldn't help reaching for the sleeve of Spencer's coat as the black-haired reporter approached. "How many months did it take your task force to capture Brian Elliott?" He stuffed his notebook and pen into the pockets of his insulated jacket. "And what kind of progress are you making on capturing his accomplice, The Cleaner?"

"Gabriel Knight, *Kansas City Journal*. I assume you already know Miss Austin, or you wouldn't be here." Spencer's arm eased back against Bailey's hand as he made the introduction, almost inviting her to hang on to his unflappable strength if she needed to.

Bailey curled her fingers into the wool but fought for a bit of independence by stepping up beside him. "Why aren't you two with the other reporters?" she asked.

Vanessa Owen answered. "Because the story's here."

Gabriel Knight agreed. "I've heard all of

Elliott's claims of innocence. I'm more interested in knowing who's going to finally shut him up."

"Eloquent as always, Gabe," Vanessa sneered.

Tension bunched in the muscles beneath Bailey's hand, but Spencer's authoritative tone never changed. "If you two want to talk KCPD business, you contact me or the task force press liaison, Kate Kilpatrick. If you want specifics on how Dwight Powers is going to prosecute Elliott, talk to him. Victims have a right to privacy. Leave Bailey Austin out of it."

Gabriel Knight shook his head. "You're betting all your cards on the story of a poor little rich girl, Detective?"

"Excuse me?" A story? Did he think for one minute that her words would be any less true than what he wrote in his paper?

"I'm not a gambler, Mr. Knight." Spencer cut Bailey off before she could organize her thoughts into a protest. He laid his gloved hand over hers where it clung to his arm. "I'm putting all my faith in the truth."

Spencer's adamant defense was just as surprising as the insult to her character and reliability had been, catching Bailey off guard. She looked up to gauge the sincerity of his words, the meaning behind his touch. But the profile of his clenched jaw revealed nothing.

The reporter lifted the camera that hung from his neck and snapped a picture. "Can I quote you on that?"

When Spencer refused to answer the taunt, Gabriel Knight nodded, lowering his camera and accepting détente, for now. "I wish you the best of luck next week, Miss Austin. The department could use it."

Apparently, Vanessa Owen needed to have a last word, too. "We'll be at the courthouse next week, Detective. You can't keep your girlfriend away from us forever."

Girlfriend?

Vanessa's gaze dropped to the spot where Bailey's hand nestled beneath Spencer's, daring him to deny the gossipy enticement. But he didn't say another word.

"She's right." Breaking the tense silence, Gabriel Knight offered Bailey a wink. "I'll see you at the Christmas Ball this weekend. I get to escort my boss to the event to help cover a feel-good story for the holidays."

"You're coming…?" Bailey felt the winter chill seep through her coat.

Of course there'd be reporters at the event. Her mother counted on the publicity to generate more donations after the fact, while the big donors at the ball appreciated the positive press. But she'd foolishly expected them to focus on the needs of the children's hospital wing or the award-winning holiday decor, evening gowns and tuxedoes. She hadn't counted on a hard news man like Gabriel Knight to be there.

"See you then." Knight nodded to his competition. "Vanessa."

"Gabe."

Both reporters walked to their cars and drove away before Spencer abruptly released her. Bailey tried to smooth the wrinkles she'd left on his sleeve, but he moved away to open the car door for her. Wondering if she should apologize for clinging to him again, yet worried he'd tell her the needy grabs were proof that she wasn't emotionally ready to testify, Bailey chose to address the two reporters. "Gabe Knight is an antagonistic, unpleasant man. It almost sounds as if he's got some beef against the police department."

"I don't know what Knight's problem is. He's always been critical of the department. And Vanessa Owen's an ambitious, opportunistic—"

"She's not a lady?"

"Something like that." He gestured to the seat behind the wheel and Bailey dutifully climbed inside. "Don't let him corner you at that ball, all right? You don't have to talk to him."

Bailey buckled her seat belt and turned on the heat. "What about the other reporters? At the very least, Mother will want them to take a family picture."

"Pictures are fine. And you can talk to the other guests. Just don't say more than 'Merry Christmas' or 'Where's your checkbook?' to anyone." He reached into his jacket and pulled out his cell phone as he stepped back. "You've got my card, right?"

She flashed it from her coat pocket before tucking it back inside. "Wait a minute." She could talk to the other guests? Bailey tilted her head up to the detective who was punching a number into his phone. "Mr. Knight's boss is the editor of the *Kansas City Journal*. She'll be there Saturday night. The editor is Brian Elliott's ex-wife, Mara Boyd."

"And she posted Elliott's bail." Spencer waved his phone, letting her know he'd already made the connection. "If she's willing to post a half-million-dollar bond for the man she divorced, then she may be willing to do a lot more."

Was Brian Elliott's ex-wife The Cleaner? Or was she being blackmailed into helping her ex like so many of The Cleaner's accomplices had done? And if Mara Boyd-Elliott showed up at her mother's fund-raiser this weekend, should Bailey avoid the woman or ask what the hell she was thinking by helping such a vile, violent man? Or maybe she could find out if Mara needed some kind of help to get away from him?

"Bailey." Granite eyes demanded her attention. "Leave the detective work to me," he warned, as if reading her thoughts. "You just show up at the courthouse Monday morning. Remember the rules and stay safe." He grabbed the car door as he put the phone to his ear. "Hey, Nick. I need you to run a check on—"

He pushed the door shut and waited for her to lock it before he strode away, turning his attention to his partner on the phone. But when he stopped at the elevator, he faced her again, pulling back his coat to prop a hand at his waist, continuing his conversation—completely impervious to the winter air or sneaky reporters or eyewitnesses who wouldn't go away.

Do what you're told. Let someone else handle the tough stuff.

Understanding the unspoken message in his watchful gaze better than she wanted to, Bailey shifted the car into Reverse and backed out of her parking space. Reluctantly, she drove around the pillar and down the ramp to the garage's lower level, losing sight of that beacon of red-gold hair and the man who'd taken over her life for the past hour or so.

The weather looked far more drab, her world felt far more lonesome, than it had just a few minutes earlier. Spencer Montgomery irritated her with his cool, emotionless obsession with duty. But it was that same undeniable strength and grace under pressure that she had clung to when she'd been afraid or unsure of herself this morning.

Bailey braked at the garage's exit and waited for traffic to pass. She couldn't help glancing at the stairwell and elevator, wondering if she'd catch another glimpse of the man she found so compelling. But the street cleared and Bailey pulled out, leaving the fireworks of her time spent with Spencer Montgomery behind.

She shook her head at the irony of being attracted to a man who held himself in such control. During the time she'd spent in Spencer's company, she'd felt anger, security, frustration, strength, uncertainty, excitement and fear. In short, everything a normal woman should feel.

But that was the curse of her life, wasn't it? Until the trial was finished and Brian Elliott was behind bars permanently, she had no real chance at *normal*.

Chapter Four

Bailey shoved open the front door of the restored 1910 brick office building that had looked so charming an hour ago and hurried away from the suffocating atmosphere inside.

Not even the blast of cold through her coat or the swirling snowflakes that stuck to her hair and melted against her cheeks could temper the frustration brewing inside her. The heels of her leather boots clicked a quick staccato down the salted concrete steps until she crunched into the pristine layer of new snow masking the half-frozen slush and grimy cinders in the parking lot.

Her face ached with the smile she'd glued on her face, and for what? The executive she'd just met with was probably trading blonde jokes with his assistant right now. Imagine, thinking heiress Bailey Austin really wanted to get down in the trenches and work like any other young woman eager to launch a meaningful career.

Bailey pulled her sunglasses from her purse to protect her eyes from the brightness reflecting off the white landscape of cars and concrete. She trudged toward the row of denuded dogwood trees, their branches brushed with snow and decorated with clear Christmas lights. The decorations had made her festive and hopeful an hour ago. Now they were simply a bunch of trees that separated the parking lot from the street, reminding her how far away from the building she'd had to park—and how the long walk and the anxious nerves had all been a waste of time and emotional energy. The end result of her job interview was the same as it had been last week, and two weeks before that.

No experience? No chance.

Apparently, she had only one thing going for her. And that was only because her mother had married a wealthy man.

Bailey punched the remote engine start on her key fob and grumbled against the wrap of her navy wool scarf, mimicking the foundation chairman she'd left upstairs. "We're so pleased the Mayweathers are interested in our museum." Bailey unlocked her car as she approached, dropping her voice to its regular pitch. "But you're not interested in *me,* are you?"

She opened the door to drop her purse on the front seat and retrieve the windshield brush and scraper. When she slammed the door, a glob of snow and slush plopped onto the pointy toes of her boots. Feeling the ultimate indignity, she turned her face to the upper window of the office where she'd interviewed. "All you're interested in, Mr. Stern, is Jackson's checkbook."

The accusation traveled up into the air on a warm cloud of breath, dissipating far more quickly than the emotions simmering inside her. Turning her attention to the necessities at hand, Bailey brushed the snow off the windshield and lifted the wiper to scrape away the icy bits that had frozen underneath. The physical exertion stretched her muscles and deepened her breathing, giving her an idea of where she'd head to next instead of finishing up some Christmas shopping as she'd planned. Her trauma counselor had recommended regular physical activity to combat any signs of depression or post-traumatic stress. These bursts of frustrated anger certainly qualified as a symptom of PTSD. Bailey could tell a good workout would go a lot further than a shopping expedition toward dispelling the self doubts and helplessness that were crushing her today.

Circling the hood of her car, Bailey tackled the other half of the windshield, anxious now to get to the gym to find the catharsis she needed—to reclaim some control of her life. She felt trapped somewhere between uselessness and a mockery of the woman she wanted to be. She had to be good for something in this world besides having money and being a gracious hostess. That resumé hadn't done her a bit of good the night of the rape.

Maybe if she'd been smarter. Braver. Wiser about the world. In control of her own life. Maybe if she'd been independent enough to stand up for herself that night, Brian Elliott never would have pegged her as an easy victim.

That was the reason she had agreed to testify at his trial. The walls of helplessness and frustration that had been building up around her since the assault had grown so tall that they were collapsing in on her, burying any spirit, any self-confidence she had left. She needed to take care of herself, not be taken care of. She needed to be necessary to someone else—vital to some cause.

She'd survived that night for a reason. But beyond testifying, she'd yet to find what that reason might be. She desperately needed to find some purpose, and soon. Or she was going to go stark, raving, absolutely stinking crazy.

A bright flash of light darted across the lenses of her sunglasses, startling her like a gunshot.

"What the…?" Instinctively, she spun her back against the solid protection of the car.

A second flash turned her attention to the far end of the parking lot. She glimpsed a small circle of glass reflecting the brightness of the sun and realized it was a camera's zoom lens.

Pointed at her.

"Hey!" she called out. Seriously? Some reporter had tracked her to a job interview? Probably Vanessa Owen or Gabriel Knight trying to scoop their competition again.

It could be some version of publicity for this weekend's Christmas Ball. It wouldn't the first time a paparazzo had snapped a picture of the Mayweather heiress. But she plain old wasn't in the mood to be rich or famous or somebody else's ticket to success right now. "What do you want…?"

The dark figure, more like the blur of a shadow, ducked down behind the row of cars, pulling the camera with him. She heard a car door slam and Bailey instinctively ran to the trunk of her car and stretched up on tiptoe, trying to get another glimpse of the photographer. But there was no one to see. She couldn't even be sure which car or truck he'd gotten into.

She sank back onto her heels and glanced up and down the lane of parked vehicles. There was no movement anywhere except for the lines of traffic on the street behind her.

"Where did you go?" she whispered, backing her hip against the cold, wet fender of her Lexus. Since when did the paparazzi want a picture of her at anything other than a high-profile social event? And how did this particular photographer know who she was, all bundled up like this, or where she'd be?

"Call me if anything makes you feel nervous or you sense any kind of threat."

Spencer Montgomery's terse warning from the day before echoed in her head. She slipped her fingers into her coat pocket, closing them around his business card.

Was this a threat? Should she call the detective?

She'd been an assignment for him yesterday—and an annoying one at that. He'd delivered Chief Taylor's warning about keeping herself safe. He'd drilled it into her head more than once that she was woefully unprepared for the challenges of the trial. Spencer Montgomery didn't think she could take care of herself. But she could. She had to.

Bailey's gaze darted to the sound of an engine turning over in the distance. She had no doubt the photographer's attention had been on her. That he'd taken one or more pictures of her.

She heard wheels squealing against the pavement, burning away the snow and slush until they found traction. The noise drew her attention to the smoky exhaust rising from a black car some thirty yards away.

She watched the black roof of the sedan backing out of its parking space and turning, not toward the exit at that end of the parking lot to make a quick getaway, but down through the long lines of cars between Bailey and the building. He might be one row over, but the driver was creeping closer. He was coming toward her.

"Idiot." The air whooshed out of her lungs as sense returned. She didn't waste a moment trying to figure out the driver's identity, whether he might be someone with the legitimate press or more gossipy tabloids, or even if he was something much more sinister. Bailey dashed around the car and climbed inside, locking the doors behind her.

Take care of yourself, Bailey.

Swearing at her own foolishness, she tossed the scraper to the floor boards and squeezed her hands around the steering wheel. Counting her breaths so she wouldn't hyperventilate, she flipped on the lights and wipers and shifted her car into Reverse, repeatedly checking her side-and rear-view mirrors to track the position of the black car.

The driver hadn't reached the end yet, hadn't turned the corner to either take the south exit or come up the lane where she was parked.

Sensing some sort of short reprieve, Bailey quickly backed out of her parking space and shifted into drive, heading in the opposite direction without giving any thought to her destination. *Away* was all she had in mind. *Get away.*

Her pulse rate quickened when she spotted the car in her rearview mirror. Bright lights. Dark windows. No chance to see the driver inside.

Bailey pressed harder on the accelerator as the car behind her picked up speed. The driver hadn't exited the parking lot. He was following her. He wanted something more.

She turned a quick left toward the north exit but had to pump her brakes and slide to a stop at the beginnings of rush-hour traffic clogging the street. She needed to go left to get to her gym and apartment, and turned on her signal. But until the stoplights switched at the nearby intersection, there wasn't going to be a break in traffic.

And the black car was coming closer.

"Come on, red light." Bailey's fingers drummed against the steering wheel. She didn't even have an opportunity to turn right if she'd wanted to. All the people who weren't heading home to the suburbs were apparently eager to get to the shopping and nightlife districts near downtown K.C.

Five lanes of traffic, all blocking her escape.

"Come on." Unless she was willing to cause a wreck, she was trapped.

How long had the man in the car been spying on her? He must have been lying in wait, biding his time until she emerged from the building. How could he have known she was even coming here at all unless he'd followed her from her lunch date with her mother at the Mayweather estate to the interview? Or even longer than that? Had he been at her apartment? Did he know where she lived? Why hadn't she sensed his presence earlier?

Maybe *she* was the only thing that was off today. She'd been so angry, so unsettled by another argument with her mother and the outcome of the interview, that she'd forgotten the cardinal rule of personal safety—be aware of your surroundings. Know where you are and who's there with you. Detective Montgomery would be saying *"I told you so"* right now. She knew better. She'd let this happen.

Could there be a longer red light anywhere in the city? "Come on!"

She pounded her fist on the steering wheel. She'd been angry *that* night, too. Angry that her mother and Harper were taking over the plans for her wedding, that her future was spinning out of her control. She'd stormed away from the Fairy Tale Bridal Shop, wanting fresh air, needing time alone. She hadn't been aware of the danger stalking her until it was too late.

Maybe she *did* need someone to take care of her.

The black car was close enough that she could make out the shape of the driver, if not his face. His window was sliding down. She spotted the narrow camera lens again.

Just the flash of reflected sunshine on glass. Aimed her way.

That *was* a camera, wasn't it?

Could that be the scope of a rifle instead?

With a desperate sound that was half groan, half scream, Bailey stomped on the accelerator and fishtailed out into the nearest lane of traffic. Horns honked, cars skidded. But she managed to put three vehicles between her and the black car before the light finally turned red and she was forced to stop.

She checked her rearview mirror, then turned all the way around in her seat to verify that the black car had leisurely pulled out of the parking lot and turned left, merging into traffic and heading in the opposite direction.

Not following. Not interested. Not a gun. Not threatening her in any way.

Sinking back into her seat, Bailey closed her eyes. The relief coursing through her was so intense that it made her lightheaded.

It took another blast of honking horns to open her eyes and pull forward at the green light. Remembering the relaxation techniques Dr. Kilpatrick had taught her, Bailey breathed in deeply, in through her nose and out through her mouth. She organized her thoughts as she settled into the normal flow of traffic. Had she ever been in any danger at all? Had the only threat been inside her head? She'd been in the papers before, and probably would be again.

Perhaps her mother had even leaked Bailey's name to the press. Just like the Blue & Gold Ball a decade earlier, where she'd been presented as a debutante, Loretta's Christmas Ball would be Bailey's reintroduction to Kansas City society—and a huge publicity coup in the name of charity. The press's interest in her might be annoying, but it wasn't dangerous.

The photographer's appearance probably merited a heart-to-heart with her mother about avoiding the spotlight, not a phone call to Detective Montgomery about imminent danger. Thank God she hadn't called him. He'd probably shake his head at her paranoid imagination, blowing the perceived danger all out of proportion. If she overreacted like this any time someone showed the least bit of curiosity about her, then he was right to worry that she wouldn't make a credible witness on the stand.

And she didn't want Spencer Montgomery to worry about her competence. Tempting as it might be to surrender herself to the detective's protection, it wasn't Spencer Montgomery's job to drop everything and come to her rescue anytime something spooked her. Besides, she'd probably only look more like a child in his eyes, like that *poor little rich girl* who couldn't fend for herself Gabe Knight had accused her of being. And she definitely wanted Spencer Montgomery to think of her as a competent, capable *woman*.

Because she was thinking far too often about him—even when she didn't need a cop.

A smile curved her lips as panic dissipated and calmer, more intimate thoughts replaced her fear. Despite the difference in their ages, Bailey had felt that subtle spark of interest from the red-haired detective, just as surely as she'd felt those ribbons of heat warming her skin when he'd touched her, waking something feral and feminine inside her.

What the man lacked in warm fuzziness, he made up for in rock-solid dependability. Spencer Montgomery was a steely-eyed warrior in a suit and badge. He was all male. All mature. All the time.

He was definitely a man she could lean on. What would her life have been like if she'd been engaged to Spencer a year ago? Would she have stormed away from planning a wedding with him? Would he have allowed her to get hurt?

But even as she remembered how the detective had seen to her safety and taken care of her yesterday, Bailey was reconsidering this attraction to a man who surely only saw her as the means to finally closing his task force investigation. After all she'd been through, she got the logic of falling for a man who was such a no-nonsense protector, a man she could trust.

But what happened to taking care of herself? To asserting her own independence as part of the healing process? She didn't have time for romance right now. She wasn't sure she was ready to fall in love and be the strong, self-sufficient woman that a man like Spencer Montgomery deserved. She had so much growing yet to accomplish, so much healing left to do.

Whatever she was feeling for Detective Montgomery needed to be buried away as a schoolgirl crush on a heroic man, or her hormones finally getting over the shock of the rape and latching on to the first available male to stir her interest in more than a year.

"How'd I do, doctor?" she chided herself in the rearview mirror as if she'd been discussing her thoughts aloud with her therapist. "You tell me, Bailey," she answered, imagining Dr. Kilpatrick's kind yet challenging response.

Bailey nodded her understanding as if she were in the middle of a counseling session. "Get a grip on those emotions," she advised. "Find something meaningful, practical and tangible to do to rebuild your self-confidence and keep you too busy to second-guess every thought or action."

Winking at her reflection, Bailey took the therapist's advice to heart. "Yes, ma'am."

She was learning to trust her instincts again, to allow herself to feel emotions like fear and anger without them crippling her. Now she needed to put those rusty skills into practice.

"Meaningful." Making a decision would be a good place to start.

"I'm going to do something practical." A workout would provide both a mental and physical health benefit.

"Now, make it tangible." She shook her head at the obvious solution. How about figuring out how she was going to get to her gym for a workout now that she was driving in the opposite direction?

Her pulse settled into a normal beat as her thoughts centered and her fears calmed. She pulled into the turn lane at the next stoplight to get off the main traffic way and circle back to the tony neighborhood where her apartment and the nearby gym were located.

Bailey sat there for a couple of minutes, waiting for the light to change. She watched car after car drive past in front of her—silver cars, white cars, dirty cars, black cars. A shiver of unease rippled down her spine, despite the self-talk that had shored up her confidence.

Was that the same black car driving across the intersection? Had the photographer changed directions and tracked her down again?

Turning after the light changed, Bailey tried to block those suspicions from burrowing back into her imagination. She went on to the next through street and turned right again, heading back in the right direction, at least.

But her gaze kept sliding to her mirrors. Had the man with the camera slipped back into traffic behind her when she wasn't looking? There was another black sedan following the pickup truck behind her. And another even farther back.

One black car—no problem. Two? A silly coincidence. Three? Four? Suddenly, it was hard to tell the black cars apart. Was that driver peeking around the truck to check on her or the heavy traffic? Had that one darted into the lane behind her to avoid detection or to stay on her tail? Maybe one of the oncoming cars was the photographer searching for her again—signaling to someone else that she'd been spotted.

"Stop it." Bailey slowed at the next light and turned. "The threat isn't real," she told herself. "This is all in your head."

The truck zipped straight through the intersection and the black car turned and pulled right up behind her. But with the lights and the snow flurries, she couldn't make out the driver. Was it a man? A woman? The Cleaner was a woman. The Cleaner wouldn't want her to testify.

Bailey muttered an unladylike curse, hating the automatic turn of her thoughts. "Really? You're going make yourself scared of everything?"

To prove she was creating a problem out of nothing, she made two more random turns. But the black car stayed with her.

Was that still a coincidence?

Pressing on the accelerator, she raced through a yellow light.

The black car picked up speed and followed.

With her breath catching in her throat,

Bailey glanced into the rearview mirror. "*That's* not my imagination."

Forget her craving for independence. Forget risking embarrassment with the first man to awaken anything inside her since the rape. She had a responsibility to the D.A.'s office, the women of Kansas City and herself to fulfill. There was paranoid, and then there was stupid.

After turning onto the interstate, the busiest road she could find, Bailey pulled Spencer's card out of her pocket and reached for her phone.

Chapter Five

Spencer leaned back in his chair. "Detective Montgomery."

"I don't want you to think I'm crazy."

Odd way to begin a conversation. But he'd recognize that soft, sweetly articulate voice anywhere. He turned his mouth closer to the phone. "Bailey?"

"Yes. I know you're a busy man. But, you said if I felt… If I…" Her long pause lingered in his ear long enough for him to identify the traffic noise in the background. "I'm not sure what to do."

"Where are you?" Her gasp triggered something urgent and wary that he'd rather not feel. He sat up straight when she didn't immediately answer. "What's wrong? Bailey?"

Spencer's dark-haired partner, Nick Fensom, looked up from the desk across from him. "Problem?"

Possibly. But the woman wasn't making much sense. "What's going on?"

"My mistake," she announced abruptly. "I'm sorry I bothered you."

"Hold on." When she started to hang up, Spencer tossed the file he'd been updating onto his desk and turned his full attention to his phone. "Why did you call?"

The next pause transformed his concern into a vague irritation rising beneath his skin. Either she was searching for a good lie to tell, or the woman was addled. And he didn't believe there was a thing wrong with that brain of hers. Just as he opened his mouth to prompt an answer, her words spilled out. "There was a black car. I swear it was following me. But it just pulled off onto four thirty-five south, and I'm still headed east on seventy. And now I'm counting up exactly how many black cars are on the road. There are hundreds of them, aren't there? I probably imagined it."

To her credit, she didn't lie. But the tremulous quality in her voice told him something about the black car had spooked her. And that fear didn't sit well with him, either.

Spencer rose from his desk. "Did you see the driver?"

"Not clearly."

"Get a plate number?"

"Missouri?" That wasn't much to go on. "The angle was wrong or I was going too fast."

"And you're safe now?"

"Yes." Her laugh wasn't very convincing. "Other than surviving the perils of rush-hour traffic."

"Why did you think he was following you?" Spencer waved off Nick's sotto voce offer to call in backup.

"He wasn't. Look, I'm sorry I bothered you. It's just that there was a reporter earlier who took a picture, and I thought…" Her deliberate pause to breathe in deeply and slow her words only made him more suspicious. In his experience, there were very few random acts—sometimes, people did things without conscious thought, but there was always a reason behind the choices they made.

Bailey Austin had chosen to call him. No way was this a random mistake. "Was it Gabe Knight? Vanessa Owen?"

"I don't know. I couldn't see."

"Where are you now?"

"On my way to the gym. I figured I'd be safe with a bunch of people around, and there's always a big crowd after work." At least she had some self-preservation instincts in her. "Look, I really am trying to follow your rules, detective. But I suppose I'm still off-kilter after seeing Brian Elliott yesterday, and was projecting..."

What? Whether the cause was legit or not, there was no mistaking the fear in her voice. A fearful witness might change her mind about testifying. And Chief Taylor had charged him with making sure the woman showed up in court. "Bailey?"

"I should have thought it through before I called. My apologies. Goodbye."

"Don't—"

She'd hung up before he recognized there was something more than professional concern fueling his questions. Yeah, he was a busy man. He stayed that way for a reason. But he was also a cop, and when someone was scared, his instinct was to respond to the threat. To find the source of that fear and negate it. He didn't need Chief Taylor to give him that order.

Even if Bailey Austin hadn't intended to call him, Spencer was the man who'd answered.

And now he was the man walking through the front doors of a popular workout franchise to see with his own eyes that the witness who could put the Rose Red Rapist away forever wasn't in any real danger.

After identifying himself at the front desk, Spencer clipped his badge to the top pocket of his wool coat and pushed through a second set of doors to locate Bailey. It hadn't taken much detective work to track down the gym where she was registered, but she'd been right about the crowd. Judging by the size and popularity of the place, it'd take a stroke of luck to find her here.

He scanned the rows of men and women walking or jogging on treadmills and stair-climbers, searching for the chin-high blonde with stylishly short layers of sunny-gold hair. He swept through the weight room, taking note of anyone more interested in a cop strolling through than he should be.

No reporters. No TV cameras. No one who looked out of place.

He found Bailey in the back of the work-out center, wearing gray yoga pants, a pink tank top and fingerless gloves as she pummeled a heavy punching bag. Spencer's concern eased considerably, seeing her in one piece. But then he got close enough to hear how hard she was breathing, and see the vee of perspiration that darkened the back of her top. Every punch, every muttered word, told him she was working through some visceral emotions that he rarely indulged.

"Stupid." Smack. "Curator." Punch. "Wouldn't even give me—" Left, right, left, right.

"So how was that interview?"

Bailey gasped when he announced his quiet approach. She slipped halfway behind the heavy bag, holding it between them, hiding from the thing that had startled her. Her big blue eyes locked on to his, then narrowed as her initial fear dissipated and her flushed skin cooled to its natural color.

"Why don't you wear a bell around your neck?" Bailey chided him, wiping at her parted lips with the back of her wrist.

Her small, firm breasts rose and fell as she calmed the deep breaths of exertion and surprise. Her porcelain skin glistened, and even in those modest workout clothes, he could see she was built slim and sleek like a racehorse. She looked at lot different than the demure sweater-and-pearls lady who'd clung to his hand at Precinct HQ yesterday. How could a skinny, sweaty society debutante like Bailey Austin be so hot?

Oh, hell no. As soon as the electricity humming through his body registered, Spencer glanced away, burying his primal reaction to an unexpectedly sexy woman beneath a cool sweep of their surroundings. As oblivious as she'd been to his arrival, was she equally unaware of the curious weightlifters watching to see what the cop wanted with her? Or the wannabe boxer with the straying eyes sparring with a punching bag just a few feet away? A pointed look from Spencer earned an apologetic wave and turned the younger man's interest away from the curve of Bailey's backside.

Seriously? Now he was making some kind of proprietary claim? Although he'd like to think he was simply acting like a cop, defending an innocent woman from a sneaky leer, Spencer was honest enough to identify the latent attraction simmering between him and Bailey—and smart enough to know nothing should ever come of it.

Pulling back the front of his coat and jacket, Spencer slid his hands into his pockets and offered her a nonchalant shrug. "Instead of me wearing a bell, why don't you be more aware of what's going on around you?" he countered. "You need to know when people are approaching you. Or following you through traffic."

"That was a mistake." A delicate fist against the leather bag punctuated her irritation. She pointed a warning finger at him before going to task with the bag again. "I told you that on the phone."

"You did." *Take note, Montgomery.* Bailey's emotions, bubbling so close to the surface, were all the evidence he needed to remind himself that she was not relationship material for him. Not only was she younger than the women he usually dated, she was the prime witness in the case that could make his career and put him on the fast track to making captain—if not chief or commissioner one day. But most importantly, as the survivor of a violent crime, she needed the kind of sensitivity and empathy that a man so distanced from his own emotions could never offer.

"So why are you here?" she asked.

He let the cop in him do the talking. "Because you *did* call. I'd like to know why."

The rhythm of her dancing hips stuttered and she dropped her fists to her sides. "Your card was right there, in my pocket. I punched the number in before I thought it through. Everything turned out to be just fine. I got here safely. I hope I didn't take you away from anything important."

"I'm off the clock."

"Oh, so now I'm intruding on your personal life, too. Sorry."

Considering he didn't have a personal life, it wasn't much of an inconvenience. "Why do you assume that you made a mistake? Maybe that reporter *was* following you, and simply turned off when he reached his exit or once he realized you were on to him."

"Is that supposed to make me feel better? No, I'm not crazy, but yes, someone *is* after me?"

Watching the fire drain from her posture shouldn't be nudging at that locked up door inside him that wanted to care about someone again. Ignoring the impulse, Spencer easily fell back on the skills that made him such a successful investigator. Instead of offering her some meaningless reassurance, or asking her directly about the car she'd mentioned, he invited her to talk about something else. Just to get her talking. Because he didn't believe for one minute that she'd contacted him by mistake. Despite her assertion that everything had turned out "just fine," something had spooked her. And he wasn't about to risk the successful outcome of his task force investigation on the chance that a man taking her picture was a perfectly innocent coincidence. "Tell me about your interview today."

She made a decidedly unladylike scoffing noise. "It was a joke."

"So you didn't get the job?"

"No." Spencer stepped onto the mat when she turned to the bag again to vent her frustration. "Mr. Stern asked how much Jackson would donate if I took the PR position. As if my stepfather has to buy me a job. I think that was the only reason the foundation would even consider hiring me." Breathless from the exertion, she stopped punching and tilted those azure eyes up to his, frowning. "He didn't even ask about my work experience. Not that I have much except for some retail jobs when I was in college. He barely looked at the portfolio of campaign projects I created during my senior internship. The only qualification he was interested in was Jackson's money. I love my stepfather dearly, but..."

One more punch punctuated her wounded self-esteem. And though the petulant action reminded Spencer of the pampered society princess he'd once pegged her to be, there was something about the trembling line of her jaw tilting upward that spoke of depth and determination, something about the squaring of her shoulders that spoke of a fatigue that went beyond the physical exertion of an intense workout. This wasn't the same woman he'd known before her assault. That woman had been beautiful, sharp-witted, oh-so-young and off-limits. This Bailey was layered, mysterious, all grown-up...interesting.

Sexy and complex—a dangerous one-two punch for a man who didn't do relationships. He inhaled a steadying breath to cool the desire firing through his blood.

He should turn around and walk away. The last time Spencer had gotten involved with a witness, the results had been disastrous. But his will was stronger than the libidinous urges sparking inside him. His obsession with seeing the Rose Red Rapist case through to the very end didn't mean he was involved with Bailey Austin. Instead, he rationalized that he was a dedicated professional who was still working the investigation. He hadn't gotten the answers he'd come looking for yet. "Why'd you take up boxing?"

Her eyebrows arched as if she suspected his random questions might have a more specific purpose. But she played along. "My trauma counselor suggested I take up some kind of exercise that would build up my strength and give me a physical outlet for my...temper." She shrugged, curving her finely sculpted lips into a wry smile. "I never even knew I had a temper. I've always been the peace-maker in my family."

That meant she'd probably downplayed her emotions for years. But a traumatic event like a rape—*or the murder of someone you loved and swore to protect,* a cruel little voice in-side him taunted—changed a person. Spencer had locked up tight, subjugated his emotions beneath logic and levelheaded thinking so that he'd never make that kind of mistake or feel that kind of pain again. But with Bailey, everything she was feeling, everything she'd once schooled beneath a ladylike facade, was rising to the surface.

Very complex. And more vulnerable to the dangers she'd face with this trial than the brave tilt of that chin let on.

Spencer shrugged out of his coat and jacket, dropping them both to the mat be-fore unbuttoning his cuffs and rolling up his sleeves.

This was not why he'd answered Bailey's call.

Bailey backed away a step when he ap-proached the opposite side of the heavy bag. "What are you doing?"

He needed the D.A.'s star witness to show up in court and give the testimony that would lock Elliott away in his cell forever.

He needed Bailey to be safe. If she suspected a threat, he needed her to trust that instinct and take the proper action to protect herself. Time to change this catharsis of a workout to a more focused lesson in self-defense. He steadied the swinging bag between his hands. "Where's your opponent?"

Her blue eyes narrowed with confusion, but didn't look away.

Spencer leaned in closer to her. "If this bag is the schmuck who interviewed you, how tall is he?"

"Schmuck?"

"Clearly, he missed your...passion...for the job. If he didn't recognize your hunger for making an impact on his organization, then he's clearly a schmuck." When she grinned at his sardonically worded support, he felt like some kind of hero. Spencer quickly squelched the warming sensation that made him smile in return, and got down to business. "Now, where would he stand if this bag was him?"

"You really think that man was following me today, don't you?" she challenged. "That it wasn't just some paparazzo getting the scoop on Mother's Christmas Ball. The D.A. promised that I'd remain an anonymous witness until the trial begins. No one outside that look-at room yesterday knows I'm testifying."

"Brian Elliott knows. At least two members of the press do."

What color was left in her porcelain skin drained away. "You really do suck at pep talks, don't you?"

Spencer dipped his head closer to hers, dropping his voice to a whisper. "I'm a cop, not you're therapist. I don't see any point in sugarcoating the truth. If you felt there was a threat, then there probably was. Vanessa Owen is notorious for sensationalist reporting. Elliott or his attorney could have leaked your name to the press. He might have contacted The Cleaner to throw a scare into you. There are any number of possible scenarios to explain that man following you. Trust your instincts. Don't take chances."

"Take care of myself," she whispered.

"Yes." Once he realized he was close enough to count the shades of blue in Bailey's upturned eyes, Spencer abruptly pulled back and braced the heavy bag against his shoulder. "Let's start by learning a few rules of self-defense. Now, how tall was Mr. Stern?"

"I guess about there." With a nod, she shook off the hushed stupor that seemed to have temporarily claimed her, too, and pointed to the bag. "Taller than me. Shorter than you."

"Let's focus that temper so it does you some good." He gave her a quick lesson in hand-to-hand combat. "You need to punch higher or lower than where you've been aiming. Go for the throat or up his nose, or the soft gut or between his legs. You'll only hurt your hand if you punch him in the jaw or sternum like that."

"I thought I was working out my frustration." She slid back into a boxer's stance with her fists raised.

"Nothing wrong with that. But let's make every punch or kick count." He pointed to her targets and steadied the bag for her. "Try it. Nose, neck, gut or groin."

She followed his instructions with soft punches to get the placement of the blows right. He encouraged her to do it again, harder, faster, until he could feel the impact of each blow stinging him through the bag.

"Now kick him where it counts." She gritted her teeth and lifted her knee, slamming the bag against him with a feral grunt and knocking Spencer back a step. He released the bag and raised his hands in surrender, grinning. "You're a quick study. Trust me, I'm down. Or at least disabled enough that you can run away."

The admission made her smile between her

panting breaths. "You made that seem easy, like I could really do it if I had to."

He pulled down his sleeves and buttoned his cuffs. "I suppose in real life the bag would fight back."

She laughed at the lame joke. "Next time a punching bag attacks me, I'll feel better prepared. Thanks." She picked up her towel from the corner of the mat, giving him a view of a sweetly rounded backside that warmed a lot more than his ego.

But when she straightened, the pensive vulnerability shadowed her eyes again, reminding him that his hormones had no business noticing anything about the fragile beauty. Bailey Austin was a job. A witness to be protected. A means to an end. Period.

"There are very few people who expect me to be able to do anything meaningful on my own, detective. That's one reason I agreed to testify. I led a charmed, sheltered life before the attack. And afterward..." She dabbed at the perspiration on her forehead and neck. "I feel like a useless bit of fluff most days. My family treats me with kid gloves. My ex tries to fix everything for me. I make my friends uncomfortable, and they never share any of their problems with me because they think I can't handle anything negative or difficult anymore. If I lose my temper, people put up with it—if I cry, they try to appease me. If I panic over a reporter stealing a picture of me..." Her gaze dropped to the middle of his chest as her voice trailed away.

"Then the cops come calling."

"Something like that. I want to stand on my own two feet. I want to make a difference. I want..." She looped the towel around her neck and reached for him. Spencer's breath caught as her fingers settled at the front of his shirt. "Your tie's crooked." As rare as it was to catch him off guard, her firm touch surprised him. Spencer held himself still while she straightened the knot of his tie and smoothed his collar. "See? This is what I'm good for. A useless bit of fluff."

He surprised himself by catching her hands when she would have pulled away. At her startled gasp, he splayed her fingers against his chest and held them there, waiting for her questioning gaze to meet his.

"What you're doing is incredibly brave. A lot of people won't understand what facing your attacker can cost you. You may not even fully understand the repercussions of standing up against Elliott." He understood the emotional turmoil of all she was dealing with far better than she could imagine.

"Post-Traumatic Stress Disorder is a lot like grief. It manifests itself in different ways for different people. Some get angry. Some fall into a depression. It robs some people of their self-confidence and ability to make a decision while others grit their teeth and plow through life as though…" Ah, hell. Like a blind-side sucker punch, anger and despair roiled up inside him. "…as though nothing ever happened."

Bailey frowned at the tightness creeping into his voice. "You?"

Ellen Vartran's chocolate-brown eyes suddenly filled his vision, and his fingers burned with the memory of her blood seeping between them. He'd forgotten the job for a few hours and followed his heart. He'd been outgunned and outmanned, but still, the mistake had been his. And Ellen had paid the price.

"Detective Montgomery? Spencer?"

The brand of ten gentle fingertips dug into the skin beneath his shirt, chasing the horrific memory from his thoughts.

He willfully squeezed the heart-wrenching guilt from his mind and met Bailey's compassionate gaze. "I've dealt with PTSD, too."

"What happened?"

The tenderness he hadn't asked for broke a chunk off the emotional armor that kept him sane. Ah, hell. Lusting after Bailey Austin was one thing. But feeling something for her? Drinking in her caring like some kind of antidote for the guilt he carried inside him? Before anymore of his strength crumbled into dust, Spencer pulled her hands from his chest and moved away to pick up his jacket. "I'm a cop. I see a lot of stuff."

"I thought you meant something personal..." Way too personal. She'd zeroed right in on his Achilles' heel. He shrugged into his jacket, making sure she got the full view of his back while he erased whatever had tipped her off from his expression. "See what I mean?" Sarcasm seeped into her sweet voice. "No one thinks I can handle anything."

Jerk. Now he could add regret to the things he felt around this woman. Time to dial it back a notch with Bailey Austin and remind himself he was a cop on a call here, not a man who cared about a woman or who needed one to care about him. He spun around to face her again. "Tell me about the car that followed you."

Really big jerk. It was no use apologizing, either. The damage had already been done. With a stiffness to her posture that hadn't been there before, she circled behind the bag to retrieve her water bottle.

"Right. Forgot you were the relentless detective there for a minute." She peeled off her gloves and took a long drink, struggling to rein in her feelings as neatly as he'd boxed up his. "Give me a chance to shower and change first."

"I'll wait."

BAILEY WALKED AWAY from Spencer Montgomery feeling all kinds of hot and bothered. He'd seemed so solid, unflappable, patient—that it had felt natural opening up to him and sharing what she was really thinking. And then his eyes had darkened and grown distant and pain had radiated off him in waves. She'd been as drawn to that surprising revelation of humanity as she'd been to the hard warmth of his chest.

But the moment she'd dared to act on the personal connection humming between them, he'd shut her down and pushed her away. Bailey had run a gamut of emotions from surprise to wounded fury, from self-doubt to invigorating confidence, from caution to concern, from suspicion to that inevitable awareness she felt whenever the stoic detective turned those steel-gray eyes on her.

The tepid shower beating down on her skin

helped cool the embarrassment of mistakenly thinking he cared about her on some personal level. Although the raw memory she'd read in his shadowed eyes and taut voice indicated that they at least shared a familiarity with personal tragedy. The hurt she'd felt at his abrupt dismissal of her concern for him eased with the reviving scent of the citrus shampoo she massaged through her hair. And by the time she was stepping out of the locker room shower and wrapping a fluffy white towel around her body, she was breathing normally again.

Detective Montgomery had come here as a courtesy in response to her frantic phone call. His concern for her safety might only be professional, but it was genuine. And she couldn't fault the man for wanting to keep their relationship strictly business when he'd just spent more time listening to her troubles and offering a constructive way to deal with her emotions than her fawning ex-fiancé or her drama queen of a mother had.

After sliding into her flip-flops, Bailey cinched the towel together over her breasts and hurried back to her locker. The first thing on her agenda was to apologize for wigging out on the red-haired detective. The second thing was to answer whatever questions he needed her to.

Bailey set her shower caddy down on the bench beside her workout clothes and twisted the combination to open up the locker's metal door. With a quick glance at the mirror inside, she finger-combed her short hair into place, then reached for the bag of clean clothes she stored on the bottom shelf.

Her fingers froze before touching the quilted strap. She curled them into a fist, she drew back to her stomach as she tried to make sense of the three photos resting on top of her bag. The black-and-white prints were small enough to be stuffed through the air vents of the locked door, she thought obliquely, studying the images scattered over her things.

Images of her. Brushing snow off the windshield of her car. Staring daggers up at the window of the CEO who'd interviewed her. Clinging to the steering wheel of her Lexus, looking afraid.

These pictures had been taken just a couple of hours ago.

That man *had* followed her.

And he wasn't any reporter.

Her face had been crossed out in two of the photos. And on the third, scrawled in thick ink across the black-and-white image, she'd been sent a message that was frighteningly clear.

Your family will be sending out funeral notices instead of Christmas cards if you testify.

Bailey huddled inside her towel. Her blood ran as cold as the weather outside. She wasn't safe at all. Not in her car. Not here at the gym. Not anywhere.

"Detective Montgomery?" she murmured, waiting for her brain to shove aside that sense of violation so she could connect the dots. The Cleaner had found her. The woman protecting the man who'd raped Bailey had followed her, watched her, touched her things. The Cleaner had been right here, standing where Bailey now stood. She shuffled away from the ugly threat. The back of her bare knees hit the bench, startling her past the fear. She turned and shouted, "Detective? Spencer! Spence!"

She heard the startled yelps and high-pitched protests before she heard the running footsteps. A woman's voice reprimanded the locker-room intruder. "You can't bring that in—"

"Bailey?" The tall, red-haired detective swung around the end of the row of lockers. Spencer's gun was drawn and down at his side, his gray eyes fixed on her as his long strides carried him straight to her. "What happened?" he ordered, closing his free hand around her bare arm and turning her to face him.

Bailey angled her head toward her locker and he followed her gaze. "I didn't imagine anything."

"Son of a bitch." He loosened his grip and smoothed his hand up and down her arm, chasing away the chill on her skin. His sharp gaze took in everything around them before coming back to her. "You're all right?"

She nodded.

"Say it. I need to know you're not in shock."

Bailey nodded again. "I'm okay."

"Stay put." In a rapid efficiency of movement, he released her entirely, ordered the curious crowd of half-dressed women to vacate the locker room, pulled a cell phone from his jacket and punched in a number. She could hear him talking to his partner, interrupting some kind of family event, while he stalked up and down the rows of lockers, sinks and showers, making sure no physical threat remained.

Bailey was still standing there in her towel, shivering from the inside out, when he finally returned. His gaze zeroed in on hers, reassuring her, assessing her, as he holstered his weapon and spoke into the phone. "Yeah, Nick. It had to be within the past two hours. Probably not even that long. Elliott's accomplice was here—or someone she hired or blackmailed, at any rate."

Spencer held out his hand as he approached, and for one dumbfounded moment, Bailey didn't understand what the gesture meant. But when he folded his long arm around her and pulled her into his chest, she released her death grip on the towel and willingly aligned her body to his. She didn't mind the scratchy wool of his lapel beneath her cheek, or the rasp of his sleeve pricking goose bumps across her bare shoulders. He was warm. He was solid. He was safe.

"Just to secure the perimeter. I've cleared the room and I've got eyes on Miss Austin." His chin brushed against the crown of her damp hair as he glanced up. "There are no security cameras in here to monitor comings and goings, but I'll get a list of names from the check-in sheet at the front desk. You get Annie and her CSI team here pronto." He leaned back at the waist and Bailey lifted her head to meet that handsome gray gaze that searched her face. "She's safe." His fingers splayed and settled at the small of her back, keeping her close when she would have backed away. "Yes, I'm okay with that," he grumbled. Then, in a more normal, clipped tone, "Thanks, Nick."

After hanging up, that same hand tugged against her towel, pulling her away as if he'd just now discovered that he wanted to distance himself from her. "The task force is en route," he stated matter-of-factly. "I'll stay with you until backup arrives." He nodded to the goose bumps dotting her skin, and then shrugged out of his suit jacket. "You're cold."

Cold and scared. "It's her, isn't it. The Cleaner?" Spencer draped the lined gray wool around her shoulders, surrounding her in the warmth and starchy scent that lingered from his body, wrapping her up in a hug that reminded her of the strength of his body surrounding and shielding hers. It wasn't the full body contact they'd just shared, but she'd take it. At that moment, she needed whatever strength he was willing to offer to shore up her own. "I wasn't being paranoid. She *was* following me this afternoon."

"Someone was." He clutched the lapels together at the base of her throat, hesitating for one uncharacteristic moment. "I know they're not fresh, but can you put your work-out clothes back on? I want the lab to check everything in your locker for fingerprints or trace before you disturb any of it."

Calmed by both his consideration and straightforward explanation, Bailey dutifully took over holding the jacket, allowing him to free his hands and regain the professional distance he seemed to prefer. "I can do that." She picked up her sweaty things off the bench. "And don't worry. I still intend to testify."

"I'm learning that about you. There's some backbone to you." He surprised her by reaching out to cup the side of her neck and jaw. Tiny muscles jumped beneath her skin at the gentle contact. "You're someone different every time we meet."

His fingertips tunneled into the damp tendrils at her nape, and suddenly, she was plenty warm again. Could it be that Spencer Montgomery wasn't as detached from his emotions as he'd like to be? "Is that a good thing?" she asked.

"I don't know yet." As soon as Bailey turned her cheek into the caress, he pulled away. Some sort of inner battle he was waging etched a few extra lines into his face. "But I do know I won't let her get to you again."

Then he nodded to her clothes and the cop was back.

"Get dressed."

Chapter Six

The colorful holiday lights outlining every rooftop and spire of the Country Club Plaza reflected in Spencer's rearview mirror as he pulled into a parking space near Bailey's Lexus outside her brownstone apartment building.

Leaving his coat open to have easy access to his gun and badge, he climbed out of his SUV and locked it. The wintry dampness of the night air bit into the tips of his nose and ears, sharpening his senses as he turned a slow 360. The security here was decent enough, he supposed. Good neighborhood, home to young professionals and wealthy retirees. Well-lit street with private parking. A key pad and card-swipe lock on the front and side doors.

He wasn't thrilled with the high mountains of snow piled beside the walkways and parking lot where the pavement had been cleared.

Both impeded sight lines and offered anyone who covered his or her tracks several easy places to hide. And the snowflakes, hanging like dust motes in the air, the last gasp of this afternoon's storm, would need to be scraped from the sidewalks and drive before it glazed over into icy patches that could hinder traction should Bailey need to run or drive away quickly.

"Are you going to stand out here and freeze?" Bailey's remote beeped twice, signaling that her car was locked. "Or did you see something?" Her head swiveled around toward the street. "Is someone following us?"

"No. We're good."

A cloud of warm breath obscured her face for a moment when she turned back to face him. When the frosty cloud cleared, Spencer could see the fatigue that shadowed her eyes and the soft lines that bracketed her rosy pink lips. Part of him wanted to keep seeing the woman who was too young and ingenuous for his sensibilities. But despite the earmuffs and orange coat, Bailey's expression hinted at a knowledge of the darker side of life that could only be learned through fear and loss. "So what's the problem?" she asked.

She had a woman's mouth, Spencer observed idly. Full, soft, articulate. Like the lean curves of her body, there was little that was girlish about Bailey Austin anymore. He'd have to find some other excuse to keep her at arm's length and convince his libido that he wasn't interested in her.

He met her expectant gaze over the roof of her car, proving to himself that he could look into those changeable blue eyes and not react. "I'll walk you in."

She moved to meet him at the front of her car. "You didn't answer my question."

He settled his hand at the small of her back, urging her into a brisk walk to the front door. He took note of the number of windows lit up in the building. "Do you know all your neighbors?"

"Most of them." She pulled her key from her purse. "You didn't answer my question. Did you see something that alarmed you?"

"What floor are you on?"

"Second."

"Good. First floor apartments are easier to break into."

"Interesting fact. Not very comforting, and still not an answer to my question." They stopped at the front door and she glanced up.

Spencer avoided making eye contact this time and nodded toward the lock. He had nothing to prove to himself. He was just a cop escorting a frightened woman home. He wasn't involved. "I want to have a look around inside your apartment, too. Double-check that everything's secure."

With a sigh of frustration, she slid her card through the lock and pushed open the door. "Spencer. If there's one thing I can count on you to do is to give me a straight answer. Even if I don't like what you have to say."

He relented once they were standing on the lobby's beige-and-gold carpet, waiting for the wrought-iron elevator to make its way downstairs. "So far, everything's fine. Since we left the gym, I haven't seen any indication of anyone showing more interest in you than they should."

Except for himself.

Spencer wisely pulled his hand away from Bailey's back and unbuttoned his coat. He'd made the mistake of reaching for her more than once at the gym—making sure she was unharmed, reassuring her…reassuring himself she was okay. Touching her was a habit he could too easily fall into if he didn't keep his fingers busy with other important things, like tucking his gloves into his pockets or brushing the snow from his hair.

"That's good, right?" She wanted an explanation for his heightened sense of vigilance. "Do you think there'll be more threats?"

With only the muffled sounds of a television behind the building's thick walls to indicate that there was anyone else about, and the doors locked behind him, he had no reason to be standing this close to her. Since the antique elevator seemed to be taking its time, he headed for the stairs, and Bailey followed.

"The Cleaner will probably wait to see how you react to the first warning." He shortened his stride to take the stairs one at a time, allowing her to pass him and lead the way to her apartment. "But I don't want to take the chance that the threats escalate into something more serious."

She stopped at the door marked with a black number 10 on it. "Thank you for talking to me like I'm an adult." She inserted one key into the dead bolt lock and turned it. "It still scares me, but at least I can be prepared. I have an idea of what to expect."

"No, you don't." She wanted straight answers? "If the pictures don't scare you away from Elliott's trial, then she's going to look for other ways to intimidate you. Or save herself the trouble of a drawn-out stalking campaign and eliminate you as a witness altogether."

She paused with her key in the door knob and her face went pale. "Eliminate...?"

"Bailey?" The door to number 12 swung open and Bailey jumped. Spencer pushed aside his jacket and had his fingers on the snap of his holster before a barefoot dynamo with an oversize Park University sweatshirt and a blond ponytail stepped out, flashing a big smile and a friendly "hey" to him before turning to Bailey. "I thought I heard voices out here. I'm glad I caught you. You're home late. How'd the job interview go? And who's the tall Scotsman?"

"Scotsman...?" The color returned to Bailey's cheeks and Spencer let his jacket slide back into place over his gun. "Oh, the red hair. Hi, Corie." Bailey's wry smile met a matching one in return. "This afternoon wasn't great."

"Sorry to hear that. Next time, right?" The girl next door was a shorter, slightly younger version of Bailey, reminding him of the Bailey he'd first met a couple of years earlier. The woman nudged Bailey's elbow. "I didn't know this was date night. And all I'm doing is sittin' at home, painting my toenails. So... do I get an introduction?"

"Sorry to disappoint you, but it's not a date. Corie Rudolf, this is Spencer Montgomery."

Chatty, yes, but not unobservant. The petite blonde extended her hand, glancing at Spencer's badge. "Cop?"

"Yes, ma'am. KCPD."

Corie tapped her chest. "Accountant. Eckhardt and Galloway. Taken?"

Wow. The woman was certainly direct. But Spencer had neither the time nor the inclination to flirt. "Nice to meet you." He made a quick assessment of her natural coloring and last name. "German?"

The young blonde laughed. "Oh, you're good. And was I right about your heritage?"

Spencer nodded. "Guilty as charged."

"He's a charmer, Bails." The frown Bailey tilted his way indicated she might disagree. Good. He didn't need any more of whatever this magnetic pull was zinging between them, anyway.

"Were you looking for me?" Bailey asked, putting the kibosh on the other woman's flirty chitchat.

"Right." Corie snapped her fingers before reaching inside her front door. She returned with a small, cube-shaped package wrapped in brown paper and a shipping label. "The delivery man dropped this off at my place since you were gone."

"Hold on." Spencer grabbed the package before Corie could hand it off. "Did you order anything?"

"I've done lots of online Christmas shopping." Bailey pointed to the logo on the box. "That was one company I used."

"All right." Spencer scanned the box for a quick verification of the return address. Recognizing the online store instead of an anonymous package, he relaxed his suspicion a fraction, even if the timing of the gift bothered him. "Here."

He handed off the package and Bailey thanked her friend before turning to him. "Am I supposed to second guess everything that comes into my world now?"

"It's better to err on the side of caution." Straight talk, as promised. No charm needed for that.

"Is something going on?" Corie asked, the wattage of her smile finally dimming. "The delivery man said someone had to sign for it, so I did. I hope that was okay."

"Of course," Bailey assured her. "That's the standing agreement between us, right? Water each other's plants, pick up each other's packages. I appreciate you having my back."

"For a minute there, I thought I was in trouble." Corie's sigh of relief was audible.

Did she not know about Bailey's rape? He didn't suppose that was something that came up in casual conversation with the next door neighbor. And he had a feeling Corie Rudolf spent a lot more time socializing than keeping up with current events. "Because I'm half tempted to order some more Christmas presents so that guy has to deliver them. He was a cutie. And no wedding ring. I checked when he took his gloves off. Shameless, aren't I?"

Seizing the opportunity to keep Bailey in one safe space for a few moments, Spencer pulled the ring of keys from her hand. "Let me go in and check your place out first, while you two catch up." He spared one more look for Corie. "Keep your apartment locked in the future. And don't open the door unless you know who's on the other side."

"Yes, Officer." Corie giggled nervously at the practical advice. Then the tenor of her voice changed. "Are you sure everything's all right?"

"Detective Montgomery worked the Rose Red Rapist case," Bailey explained, keeping her far-too-personal familiarity with the investigation out of the conversation. "He's a stickler for personal safety."

"Did you know that guy's trial starts Monday? I saw a preliminary report on the news tonight. Vanessa Owen said she's got the inside..."

Spencer pushed open the door and the conversation faded. Well, Corie's monologue faded. He shook his head as the door closed behind him. Bailey definitely didn't seem too young, anymore.

But that still didn't make her the right woman for him.

After setting Bailey's keys on the table beside the front door, Spencer swept his gaze around the remodeled apartment's open floor plan, taking note of the formal dining room with a dark red poinsettia centerpiece, and the galley-style kitchen with a trio of carved wooden Santas sitting on the counter. Breathing in the fresh scent of pine, he moved into the living area. A Christmas tree, standing taller than him and four times as wide, stood in front of the two main windows. Although the lights weren't turned on, he counted several rows of clear bulbs and gold ribbon circling the pine branches. There was a white angel at the top and a dozen wrapped presents on the floor below.

"How'd you get that in here, woman?" he muttered, half admiring her determination to celebrate the season, despite all that had happened, and half worried about what kind of help she'd recruited to bring that behemoth up to the second floor.

Hopefully, she'd asked a close friend. Or someone who worked for her father. Not a stranger she'd paid and invited into her home. "Where you could plant a bug or camera, get the lay of the place, or gerry-rig one of the locks so you can come back later."

The possibilities of how easily an unseen threat could infiltrate Bailey's world got Spencer moving. He checked the locks on the windows behind the tree. The snow was undisturbed and drifting on the fire escape outside. Spencer verified that the fire escape ladder was up and locked into place and that the outside stairs only went to the floor above hers. An intruder would have to rappel if he wanted to get in from the roof.

The bathroom was tiny and windowless, and could make a passable safe room if she could find something to reinforce the flimsy lock. He checked the walk-in closet in her bedroom, glanced underneath the dust ruffle on the white mission-style bed and moved the blinds aside to secure the lock on the window there.

Spencer came out of Bailey's bedroom to find her draping her coat over the back of a chair and pulling a stool up to the kitchen's long, granite-top island. "Do I pass inspection?"

He glanced over at the dead bolt to make sure she'd locked it behind her. "A little heavy-handed with the holiday decor, but I like the steel-framed windows and that you have curtains or blinds covering all of them. No one can sneak a photograph of you here. And they're all secure. No signs of unwanted entry or that anyone's been peeking in."

"That's good." She set the earmuffs beside her purse and fluffed her sunny hair into a tousled disarray. "Not into Christmas?"

He shrugged, crossing through the apartment to join her. "Don't have the time for it."

"That's sad. Do you have parents or someone special you're at least going to spend the day with?" She sat on the stool to unzip her boots and pull them off.

"Now you're sounding like your friend Corie." When she bent over, Spencer reached out to smooth down a spike of golden hair, but drew his fingers back when she straightened. "No parents. No siblings. No..." An image of Ellen stepping out of the shower and shaking her long wet hair down her back tried to surface, but he quickly slammed the door on that memory. "No one special."

He turned to the counter and gripped the edge of the cold granite, willing the emotions that stirred up around Bailey Austin to settle back into place.

"I hit that same nerve again, didn't I." Her hand slid across the counter toward his. The muscles beneath his skin pulsed when her fingers brushed across his knuckles. When he fisted his hand, she pulled away. "Sorry."

She jumped down from her stool so abruptly that Spencer knew he'd hurt her feelings. While she set her boots on the tile by the front door, Spencer inhaled a cleansing breath. She couldn't get to him. He wouldn't let her. But he needed to make sure she wasn't so upset or ticked off at him that she'd get distracted from the things she needed to do to stay safe.

"I am invited to my partner Nick's house for Christmas dinner. They're a big family and they always make room for one more. I complimented his grandma Connie's cherry pie one time, and I've been an adopted son ever since."

Continuing the conversation was enough of an olive branch for her to come back to the counter, although he could see her purposely keeping some distance between them. "The cherry pie got through the infamous Montgomery armor, hmm?"

That armor didn't seem to be so tough today. And he placed the blame directly on those shadowed blue eyes and determined chin. "I've been known to indulge in a homemade dessert on occasion."

"You're lucky to have friends like that." Bailey pulled a pair of scissors from a jar on the counter and sat to open her package. "I apologize for Corie. I hope she didn't make you uncomfortable. She can talk the ears off a basset hound, and she's a little man-crazy—"

"You think?"

"—but she's got a good heart." Spencer slipped onto the stool beside her for a closer look as she sliced through the package's sealing tape. "It's been nice to have a friend who doesn't walk on eggshells around me. We share normal conversations about nothing and everything."

"You didn't tell her about the rape or the trial?"

"It hasn't come up. If she knows, she hasn't said anything. Maybe she's worried that the topic would make me uncomfortable. A lot of people don't mention it."

Spencer raised a skeptical eyebrow. "I have

a feeling there's very little that makes that woman uncomfortable."

Finally, the shadows receded and her lips softened with a smile. "Corie's right about one thing."

"What's that?"

She set down the scissors and lifted a red envelope and a squarish jewelry case from the box. "You can be charming when you're not trying to be all relentless cop."

"Charming?" The idea of Corie Rudolf turning all that man-hungry energy on him made Spencer a little sick to his stomach. "I was going for businesslike and authoritative. Remind me to do gruff and tough next time I see her."

The answering laugh died in Bailey's throat when she flipped open the jewelry case. Spencer rose to see what had changed her expression.

It was a man's watch. Expensive, shiny and new. And in pieces.

She set the box down and shuffled through the paperwork again. Something was off.

"Is that for your dad?" he asked. He hoped it was some careless shipping and handling that upset her.

"I didn't order a watch." She handed him the paper, then slipped her thumb beneath the flap of the envelope to pull out a Christmas card. "It says 'gift.' It's clearly addressed to me, but the sender's name isn't filled in. Who would give me a man's watch? A broken one at that. Maybe the card will explain the mix-up."

Bailey recoiled from the holiday card, and Spencer was behind her shoulder in an instant to read the message scrawled inside.

You'd better watch out
You'd better not cry wolf...
Or you'll be in pieces.

"Set the card down. Don't touch anything else." Spencer punched his partner's number on his cell.

She set the card on the counter as if it might detonate in her hand and stood. "This scares me."

"I think that's the idea."

"I mean, how long has this person been watching me? I only noticed someone this afternoon. But they couldn't have sent this today. Look at the date."

When she reached over to point out last Friday's date, Spencer pulled her away from the counter. "Do you make coffee?"

"What?"

"Do you have coffee in your pantry?"

"Of course, I—"

"Make it a full pot." He eased the urgency from his grip on her arm. He needed to only think about being a detective right now. He shouldn't be concerned with the frustration and fear flaring into her cheeks, or feel guilty about putting them there. He dropped his gaze down to her bare toes beneath the hem of her yoga pants, opting for something in the neutral zone between cop and caring. "Get something warm on your feet. Stay busy. I need to work."

With a surprising understanding, or maybe just resignation, Bailey nodded and prepped the coffee maker before disappearing into her bedroom.

While the phone rang, Spencer pulled off his coat and scarf and tossed them over the back of one of the dining room chairs. This was going to be a much longer night than he'd planned.

Nick finally picked up. The breathless laughter on the other end of the line told Spencer he'd interrupted something more than the dinner date his partner had mentioned at work. "Your timing sucks, buddy. What do you need?"

Not that he begrudged his best friend some private time with the woman he was going to marry, but business was business. "Put your fiancée on the phone."

Nick's tone instantly changed. "There's been another threat?"

Spencer glared at the mysterious package and cryptically worded message. If it wasn't for that Christmas card, he'd have excused it as a retail mistake at this busiest time of year. "It came through a delivery service. I need it processed for any trace."

"Miss Austin's apartment?" Spencer heard whispers in the background, shuffling sounds that meant Annie and his partner were already gearing up to leave.

"Yes."

"We'll be there in twenty minutes."

Two hours later, Spencer lifted his gaze from the fuzzy brown slipper boots Bailey wore to watch her rinse out the empty coffeepot and load the four dirty mugs into the dishwasher. Heeding his advice in a head-down kind of way that brought to mind her vulnerable admission that she sometimes considered herself a *useless bit of fluff,* Bailey had worked in the kitchen the entire time. She'd emptied the dishwasher, wiped down counters, swept the floor and refilled coffee nonstop while he and Nick canvassed neighbors in the building and made phone calls and

CSI Hermann processed the watch, card and packaging with her lab kit.

How could a woman with the guts to ignore her overprotective family's advice and stand up to her rapist in court ever think of herself as useless?

But now Annie was stowing evidence bags and packing her kit, and Nick was reporting that the delivery man who'd brought the package into the building was someone new. While it wasn't unusual to add extra drivers to the regular routes to make deliveries this time of year, no one in the building seemed to recognize the description of the man Corie Rudolf had given them. *Brown hair. Brown eyes. Super cute.* Nick had already put a call in to the company's local office to confirm an ID and get a picture of the man.

Spencer heard enough of Nick's report to know he wasn't going to get any conclusive answers tonight. He might as well listen to Annie's analysis and get out of here before he strayed from the neutral zone and went over to the kitchen sink to take Bailey in his arms again and tell her how much he admired someone with her courage and work ethic. He could confirm that the crown of that silky gold hair really did fit just under his chin, and that the lean muscle of that fit body curved in all the right places.

And he could completely screw up Bailey's life and this case if he gave in to the temptation to touch her again.

So he blinked her from his sight and thoughts, and turned his attention to Annie's dark brown eyes. "What can you tell me?"

"Good news?" Annie picked up the sealed bag that held the watch. "It's an expensive brand with a manufacturer's mark on the back that'll make it easier to trace to the source. We'll know if it was bought locally and repackaged, or where the retail order originated."

Spencer nodded. "So we can confirm a location. Maybe we can get a description of the sender. And the bad news?"

Annie placed the bag inside her kit and peeled off her sterile gloves. "The card is generic, from a set of boxed cards that are sold in shops across the country. Pretty impossible to track down. Preliminary handwriting analysis says it matches the photographs from this afternoon, but we've got nothing to compare the samples to. As for the rest? There are no fingerprints besides Miss Austin's and the neighbor's anywhere on the watch, case, card or packaging. No stray hairs in the tape, nothing that can identify the sender."

"So even if we get an address or phone number, which will probably turn out to be P.O. box or business, we can't prove who at that address sent it."

Nick crossed his arms and muttered a curse. "I can tell you who it's from."

The water stopped running in the sink and Bailey came to the opposite side of the kitchen island from where the rest of them stood. "What's the significance of the broken watch? Other than it *is* broken. The message would have been just as clear with something from a discount store. Does that mean The Cleaner is someone who has a lot of money?"

"I think I know the answer to that." Annie's dark eyes looked from Bailey to Nick, then up to Spencer. "But my idea's a little outside the box."

Spencer didn't need hesitation. He needed answers. "I didn't choose you for my team because you think like other people do."

Nick moved beside her to offer his encouragement. "Whatcha got, slugger?"

After a squeeze from Nick's hand, Annie answered, "It's what's not here that worries me."

"What's that?" Nick urged.

"Unless you just like to show off that you can afford an expensive watch, or you're a serious runner who's timing sprints or laps, there's not much call for a watch like this. Even if it's in perfect condition."

Bailey wrung the dish towel in her fists. "What would you use a watch like that for? What piece is missing?"

Spencer nodded an okay for Annie to answer, even though Bailey's face was already growing pale.

"The timer. I'd use it to build a bomb."

Chapter Seven

Spencer tapped his fingers on the polished walnut counter at the Shamrock Bar, and waved the muscle-bound bartender with the scarred-up face over to refill his glass with bourbon.

The neighborhood cop bar was quiet tonight—partly because of the late hour, partly because of the weather that slicked the streets and made it too cold for all but the hardiest of souls to venture outside, and partly because of the holiday season. Most people had parties with friends to go to or family gatherings to attend. At the very least, they were home watching TV specials and wrapping presents.

Spencer just had his thoughts, a criminologist's printout about what other elements besides watch parts would be necessary to complete a bomb, and a really, really bad feeling that something deadly was closing in on Bailey Austin.

Jake Lonergan, the silver-haired bruiser who was tending bar, pulled the good stuff from the top shelf, but set the bottle on the bar top without pouring. "This will be your third one, Spence. You on duty tonight?"

"No."

"Driving?"

He didn't answer that one. He'd never been a heavy drinker—well, there'd been a spell there after losing Ellen where he'd indulged more than he should. He and Nick used to trade off driving responsibilities so that the other could have a few. But Spencer and his partner didn't go out for drinks after a particularly tough shift or closing a case the way they used to. Nick spent most of his evenings with Annie now, remodeling and repainting an old house they planned to move into following their spring wedding on the baseball field at Kaufmann Stadium.

Spencer spent his nights at home catching up on reading reports, working late at the precinct office or hanging out here at the Shamrock, reflecting on the events of one day and organizing his plan for the next. It was a sane, solid routine that had kept him moving forward toward his career goals for the past five years.

But tonight, that dedication to duty just

felt lonesome. Wrong. Like he was somehow wasting his time.

"You got a case that's weighing on your mind?" Jake asked, flipping around the wrinkled diagram Spencer had spread on top of the bar. "So now you're researching explosives. Thinking of going postal on me?"

Spencer folded up the paper and tucked it inside his suit jacket. "You know, one of the things I like best about you, Jake, is that you don't stick your nose into other people's business."

Jake laughed. "You can't dent my hide, Montgomery. I can handle whatever sarcasm you dish out." He lifted the bottle in his beefy hand. "Still want the drink?"

After a nod, Jake poured him another shot. Jake Lonergan was a good man, even if there was a lot about him that remained a mystery. The man walked and talked like a cop, but didn't wear a badge, although he knew him to carry a knife in his boot. The two had become friends earlier in the Rose Red Rapist case when Jake rescued a woman from an assault Spencer's team had investigated. The fact Jake had identified the drawing as the specs for a bomb told him the big man had a lot of expertise in weaponry, despite gaps in other parts of his memory.

Spencer picked up his glass and set it back down without taking a sip. He pulled the drawing back out and handed it to Jake. "Did you ever run across a device like that?"

Jake's icy eyes skimmed over the print-out. "I'd like to say I don't remember, but yeah. It's a homemade bomb. You can get the parts online or in the right store easily enough without the purchases registering on any federal watch-group radar." He handed the paper back. "The actual explosive is the hard thing to get, but doable if you have access to demolition or construction."

"And you'd definitely need a watch like that to pull it off?"

"If you want to control when and where it goes off with any precision. Most bombers don't want to be around when the thing goes boom."

Brian Elliott had earned his millions in property development and renovation. Certainly, his construction crews and anyone who worked for them would have access to those materials. With KCPD monitoring Elliott 24/7, he wouldn't be able to put together a bomb. But who else in the circle of employees or friends around him would be willing to at least make it look like a serious enough threat to send Bailey into hiding or do something on a bigger scale to derail Elliott's trial? Could one of them be The Cleaner?

Of course, there were dozens of construction companies, big and small, in Kansas City. Another explosives source could be the munitions storage facilities and manufacturing plants dotting the area, or maybe even one of the National Guard posts or nearby military base.

There were too many possibilities, too few facts for Spencer to reach any logical conclusions and come up with a direction to steer his investigation into who had threatened Bailey—or even confirm that the anonymous gift was indeed another threat.

"I could talk to my friend Charlie Nash at the DEA," Jake interrupted Spencer's thoughts. "Maybe he could tell us if the Feds have any word on something like that going down here in the Midwest."

Spencer shook his head. "This isn't about terrorism. It's about intimidation." He returned the paper to his pocket, needing some time to fine tune a list of suspects. "I'll make some calls in the morning." Since the bartender had brought up one of the mysteries of his past, Spencer asked, "Have you given anymore thought to going back to the DEA or some other law enforcement agency?"

Jake pulled the towel from his apron and wiped down the bar in front of Spencer. "Not until this trial is over and the people who are a threat to my wife and daughter have been put away." Right. Jake had married the woman he'd rescued and adopted her baby, all in the span of a few months. "Until then, my most important job is playing bodyguard-slash-babysitter to Robin and Emma."

Bodyguard. Not a role Spencer could stomach anymore. That's why he'd left a black-and-white unit parked outside Bailey's building tonight, and was maxing out his favors to keep someone with eyes on her around the clock until there were no more threats and the trial was over. He'd focus on the investigation, on unmasking The Cleaner and the thugs she liked to hire, not the D.A.'s star witness.

"Where are Robin and Emma now?" Spencer asked, wondering how Jake could step away from guard duty if he really believed there was still a threat to his family.

He replaced the bottle behind the bar. "With Hope Lockhart and your buddy Pike Taylor."

"Wedding plans?" Pike was a K-9 officer on the task force. Was every man he knew building a home life outside of work?

Jake nodded. "Robin agreed to be Hope's matron of honor. I'm guessing Pike is out with the dog while the ladies discuss invitations or whatever's next on the list. It's turning into the biggest production I've ever been privy to. I swear to God, if they make me put on a tux…"

Spencer picked up his glass, swirling the golden-brown liquid around the bottom while his thoughts drifted back to the night he'd lost Ellen Vartran. He'd impulsively proposed to her that night, not sure if he was feeling love or lust, and not caring. They'd made love in the shower and the words had popped out.

He'd had one job—protect the witness in the safe house. And he'd failed. When his shift changed, he'd gone out to buy a ring. When he came back…he'd had no chance to save any of them.

He'd been an empty man and a useless cop for months afterward.

A useless bit of fluff.

Spencer knew exactly what Bailey was feeling right now—that driving need to do something meaningful to atone for the sins and shortcomings that ate away at a person's soul, to make a difference that might just assuage the fear and pain and guilt that tore a person apart inside.

Finding the mole who'd betrayed the safe house had been Spencer's first step toward redemption. Arresting the Rich Girl Killer had been the second. Putting Brian Elliott away for the Rose Red rapes might finally put a staunch on the emotional wound that still bled inside him.

He raised his glass to his lips, maybe sending up a prayer for inner peace at the same time.

But the image on the television screen above the bar stopped him. "Hey, Jake. Will you turn that up?"

Spencer set his drink down and leaned in to catch Vanessa Owen's pretrial update on the ten o'clock news. Although the beautiful brunette's face filled up the center of the screen, it was the still photo in the bottom right corner that drew his attention.

It was a picture of a younger Bailey at some fancy-shmancy society event on the arm of her ex, Harper Pierce. She wore long hair swept up on top of her head. The look was innocent. Disinterested. Pageantlike. Not as sexy or compelling or touchable as the Bailey he'd spent time with today was.

"Dwight Powers has made it no secret that Mayweather heiress Bailey Austin is scheduled to testify in the trial of alleged Rose

Red Rapist, Brian Elliott. As many viewers may recall, Jackson Mayweather's stepdaughter was brutally beaten and raped, just over a year ago in downtown Kansas City." Vanessa Owen's voice hushed for a moment, as if tears of compassion or outrage clogged her throat. But Spencer wasn't buying the act of a woman who'd lain in wait to corner Bailey in the parking garage yesterday morning. "This reporter has the inside scoop that Miss Austin is extremely fragile right now. She has received anonymous threats indicating she may come to some harm if she agrees to testify. While KCPD and the D.A.'s office have no official comment, the information was confirmed by Miss Austin's mother, Loretta Austin-Mayweather. As many of you know, Mrs. Mayweather's annual Christmas Ball, which has raised millions of dollars for children's charities—"

Spencer pushed to his feet and pulled out his wallet.

Bailey Austin fragile? In looks, perhaps. Maybe even in demeanor. But the woman could be made of steel if her mother, the damned reporters and the rest of the world gave her the chance she needed to succeed.

Jake muted the television. "There's not much to like about that woman, is there."

"No." Spencer threw some bills on the bar to pay his tab without touching his drink. He already wasn't thinking with a clear head if he was listening to his gut. And though he knew that could get him into trouble, it wasn't stopping him. He grabbed his coat off the bar stool beside him.

"You heading out?" Jake asked, clearing his glass.

"Yeah. I've got work to do."

A half hour later, Spencer was setting up camp on the street outside Bailey's apartment building. He'd dismissed the uniformed officer, who was glad enough to report back to HQ for a refill of hot coffee. Sipping on his own to-go cup of java, Spencer settled behind the wheel of his SUV. He unbuttoned his collar, loosened his tie and tucked his wool scarf more tightly around his neck.

The snow had stopped falling except for a few flakes dancing through the cones of light from the street lamps along the sidewalk. All the windows that had been lit up earlier in Bailey's building were now dark, including hers. Hopefully, exhaustion, at least, would allow her a good night's sleep.

Tomorrow, he'd have answers. The delivery man could be ID'd. He'd have a list of Elliott's employees and other companies in the area with access to explosives. He'd know more from the lab regarding the origin of the watch.

Tonight, he'd sit, wait, watch and make sure Bailey Austin got that good night's sleep.

Spencer squared himself in the seat so he had a clear view of both exterior doors and Bailey's bedroom window. He was cold, tired, wearing the same clothes he'd put on that morning and his legs were too damn long for this kind of stakeout.

But it was the only way he would find any peace.

SPENCER CRACKED ONE eye open as the hazy white ball of sunrise cleared the horizon and transformed the world outside his car into a glistening crystal wonderland.

He briefly considered polishing off the dregs of the ice-cold coffee in the Suburban's cup holder, then decided he wasn't quite that miserable. Instead, he stretched the kinks out of his neck and shoulders and checked his watch. He had to report for his shift in a couple of hours, so the twenty minutes he'd lost dozing in the SUV were going to have to suffice for a night's sleep. Nodding off on a stakeout also provided more evidence that he wasn't cut out for security work anymore, either.

He'd driven over here on a whim last night, trying to make amends for a past mistake he could never truly rectify. And this is what he had to show for it—nasty coffee, bleary eyes and a cramp in his right calf that just wouldn't quit.

A quick glance across the street showed a light shining behind the blinds in Bailey's bedroom window. He'd missed when that had come on. She was probably eager to get an early start on whatever meaningful activities she had planned. He wondered how she intended to make a difference in the world today—another job interview? Helping her mother with the fund-raiser?

Spencer pulled off his glove and rubbed his hand over his stubbled face and jaw, wiping off the grin forming there. Maybe Bailey's fears about the threats she'd received or a nightmare with Brian Elliott's face in it had kept her from sleeping through the night. She might be in there pacing, worrying, wondering who she could call at this time of morning.

"Ah, sweetheart," he murmured on a heavy sigh that fogged up the side window.

It took him a second to realize he'd placed his hand over his heart, above the chest pocket where he'd stowed his cell phone. "Smooth,

Montgomery," he chided himself. Boy, did he need some real shut-eye—his thoughts weren't making any sense. Wishing for a call from Bailey was asking for trouble. Spencer sat up as straight as he could and flexed his leg while he wiped the frosty moisture of his breath from the cold glass.

That's when he saw the man jiggling the handle on the building's side door. Black pants, black parka, black stocking cap on top of his head—built on the heavy side and stuck without a key to get in, judging by the way he tugged on the latch and peeked through the windows on either side of the door.

Spencer slid his hand inside his jacket to retrieve his phone to call it in. But what would he report? A resident locked himself out of the building? Maybe that was the maintenance guy who'd come out to shovel sidewalks and had forgotten his key card.

He needed to wait. Observe. Make the right decision.

After a furtive look to his right and left and the parking lot behind him, the man trudged through the knee-deep snow to the front sidewalk. He tried the same routine on the front door, twisting the handle and peeking in.

Suspicion fueled the heat traveling through Spencer's veins. He unbuttoned his coat and clipped his badge onto his outside pocket while he watched. He pulled back the edge of his jacket to have clear access to his gun and snugged his gloves into place around his fingers while his gaze trailed the man's movements around the building.

When the man gave up on easy entry at the front door, he lifted the hem of his parka. Spencer's left fingers curled around the door handle when he spotted the tan leather case attached to the man's belt. Could be a carrier for a cell phone, could be the bottom edge of a holster or sheath for a knife.

Spencer pulled the handle and inched the SUV's door open, acclimating himself to the bracing temperature outside. A quick scan up and down the street revealed no traffic, no one moving in the parking lot, no one even out to snow-blow their driveways or throw down some sidewalk salt yet. Just a lone man in a parka, possibly armed, his face half-obscured by a pair of wraparound sunglasses, prowling outside Bailey's apartment building.

The man pulled down his jacket without retrieving anything from his belt. Had he sensed Spencer's presence? Did he know he was being watched?

He was scanning the sidewalks and street now, too. But Spencer held himself still enough that the man's attention never settled on the black Suburban and the cop watching him. As if deciding the coast was clear, the man suddenly jumped off the front steps into the snow and jogged past the first window. When he moved, Spencer moved. Spencer dashed across the street and crouched down beside a parked car, pulling his gun to cradle it between his hands, controlling his breath so a big cloud wouldn't give away his location in the frigid morning air. He peered through the windows to keep an eye on Mr. Suspicious.

The guy with the sunglasses stopped at the bottom of the fire escape and kicked aside several layers of snow, clearing a space before jumping up to capture the bottom rung of the fire-escape ladder. After one more quick look around him, he pulled the ladder down and put his boot on the first rung.

Spencer was around the car in a flash. He leaped over the slush piled at the curb and broke through the top crust of frozen snow as he crossed the yard, impervious to the cold seeping into his feet and legs as he ran straight for the intruder.

"KCPD! Put your hands on top of your head!"

"What?" The man hopped to the ground and turned.

Spencer braced his feet and aimed his Glock. "Hands up!"

"Put the gun down, man." Instead of obeying the command, the man lifted the hem of his coat.

"Hands!" Spencer didn't give him a second chance. Time to move. "Face the wall."

"There's been a mistake, Officer." The guy raised one arm, but the other was moving toward his parka again. "I'm reaching for my ID."

"Yeah?" The man was younger and bulkier than Spencer, but not as tall or quick. Spencer spun him and shoved him against the brown bricks, pressing his Glock at the base of the perp's neck to keep him in place while Spencer quickly patted him down. Cell phone. Belt buckle. Ah, hell. *Mistake, my ass.* Spencer unsnapped the holster he'd spotted earlier and pulled a gun from the guy's belt. "You sure you're not reaching for this?"

Although the man was smart enough to keep his hands on the wall, he didn't give up the fight. "I've got a permit for that Sig Sauer. I'm a security guard. ID's in my front right pocket. I'm familiarizing myself with the building, making sure it's locked up tight."

After tucking the Sig Sauer into his own belt, Spencer pulled the intruder's hands behind his back and cuffed him. Only then did he holster his own weapon and pull his prisoner from the wall. "A guard who carries an FBI-grade weapon and doesn't know his own building? Is that why you were climbing up to the second floor to break in?"

"I wasn't breaking— Hey!"

The so-called security guard swore when Spencer took off his sunglasses and pushed up the edge of his stocking cap. Brown eyes. Brown hair. He fit the vague description of the man who'd delivered Bailey's package yesterday. "Is this your first time here—" he read the name on the ID he pulled from his pocket "—Mr. Duncan?"

"You can read what it says, can't you? Zeiss Security? Max Duncan?" The dark-haired man tried a taunting glare that might have worked on someone else. Spencer wasn't in the mood. "I'm legit. Now unlock these things."

"You didn't answer my question." Spencer stuck the ID back into Duncan's parka. If Duncan *was* his name. Annie Hermann had nearly been killed by a man working for The Cleaner, a man who'd been impersonating a police officer to gain access to one of the Rose Red Rapist's crime scenes. He wasn't taking a chance on being fooled twice by the same M.O. He pushed the alleged Max Duncan through the snow to the front door. "I don't know you, pal. Until I get some answers I like, I don't care who that billfold says you are."

Max jerked his arm from Spencer's grip and climbed the front steps himself. "Buzz apartment ten. She'll vouch for me."

Bailey's apartment? Not likely. Spencer pushed the button to number twelve, instead.

"Yes?" a sleepy voice answered after the third buzz.

Spencer grabbed Duncan's wrists behind his back and twisted just enough to remind the man who was in charge here. "Miss Rudolf? This is Detective Montgomery from KCPD. We met last night?"

"Ooh, yes. The ruddy Scotsman who *isn't* dating Bailey." Her drowsy voice perked up and the door unlocked. "Come on up."

Gritting his teeth against the flirty subtext of her invitation, Spencer pushed Duncan inside and followed him up the stairs.

"I tell you my name's Duncan," Spencer's prisoner protested. "Call my boss, Mr. Zeiss. I'm running security here. That ID is legit."

"One question first."

Corie Rudolf opened her door as they crossed the landing, foolishly forgetting his

warning to identify any guest before unlocking her door. "Hey, Detective. You're here bright and early." Her friendly greeting chilled and she pulled her pink flannel robe together at the neck as she looked up at Max. "And you brought company."

Was that a glimmer of recognition in her eyes?

"Is this the man who delivered Bailey's package to your apartment yesterday?" Spencer asked. "Have you seen him before?"

"Maybe?" she answered after a moment's hesitation. Her eyes darted to Spencer, making him wonder if he should trust her answer. Was she just saying what she thought he wanted to hear? But suddenly she was chatty again. "Yes. Yes, he is. Where's your uniform? That kind of threw me off. Did you have another package for me?" She thrust out her hand and smiled. "We didn't get a chance to officially meet before. I'm Corie."

Duncan eyed her extended hand, rattled his handcuffs and shook his head. "Lady, you and I—"

The dead bolt turned in the door to apartment ten and Spencer shifted to put himself between Bailey and his prisoner.

"Spencer?" She appeared in the crack of the open door, wearing a pair of black pants and a lime-green jacket, with a towel wrapped around her head. Fresh out of the shower and in the middle of dressing, he guessed, judging by the towel on top and her bare feet below. She peeked over the chain at the dark-haired man beside him and frowned. "Max?" She closed the door to quickly unhook the chain and then swung it open. "What are you doing here? Are those handcuffs?"

"Miss Austin. Your stepdad sent me over to keep an eye on you." Max pushed against Spencer's hand, but he wasn't budging. "You want to tell this butthead cop that I'm on your side?"

Bailey's mouth opened, then closed. Then she inhaled a quick breath. "It's okay, Spence. Max works for Zeiss Security. They work for Jackson."

"You're not the delivery guy?" Corie reached across the gap between the doors to squeeze Bailey's hand. "Are we in some kind of danger? Bails, what's going on?"

"Read the news sometime, Corie." Spencer's red-haired temper rarely surfaced, but he was too tired to keep from snapping.

"Excuse me?"

"Spencer." The gentle reprimand from Bailey surprised him.

Those blue eyes searching his for some

kind of explanation quickly defused his raw impatience. "My apologies."

Several silent seconds passed while she took in his disheveled state, wet shoes and sour mood. Then she patted Corie's hand and smiled. "Sorry if we woke you. You're perfectly safe. I've…been working with the D.A.'s office on a project and…Detective Montgomery is helping me. Max is…an old friend. Go back to bed. I promise I won't let these two argue anymore."

"Well, I didn't really mind. I'm just glad everything's okay." The two women traded a hug before Corie retreated into her apartment with a winsome smile. "Nice to meet you, Max."

After the door locked on apartment twelve, Bailey led the two men into her apartment and closed the door behind them. She walked straight past them to the kitchen, pausing to nod toward the cuffs on Duncan's wrists. "Unless you're arresting Max, those aren't necessary."

Spencer pulled out his keys to unlock the handcuffs.

"Thanks." Max nodded to her and pushed his wrists toward Spencer.

"You didn't know Duncan was coming?" When she shook her head, Spencer closed the key in his fist and pointed to her phone. "Call your stepdad to confirm his assignment."

Max swore.

Bailey pulled the towel off her head and combed her fingers through her hair. "Are you going to tell me what's wrong?"

Spencer stood firm. "I'm a stickler for details. Make the call."

Five minutes later, Spencer had his answer, along with a throbbing headache behind his eyes and a nagging skepticism that there was still something wrong with this whole scenario. Either Max Duncan wasn't who he said he was or Corie Rudolf was lying. They couldn't both be right. And both of them were too close to Bailey for him to feel comfortable about any of this.

"Did you deliver a package to Corie Rudolf yesterday?" Spencer asked, unhooking the handcuffs.

Once he was free, Duncan faced Spencer, rubbing his wrists and looking like he wanted to punch him. "My gun?"

"My question?"

Understanding who had the upper hand here, the stocky man pulled off his cap and waved it toward the adjoining wall between apartments. "I have no idea what that crazy woman was talking about. If I look like somebody she's supposed to know, that's on her. My boss told me to provide some extra security for Jackson Mayweather's stepdaughter. I'm supposed to shadow Miss Austin and keep an eye on her place today. I was familiarizing myself with the layout of the building and testing its access points when you went all Dirty Harry on me."

What he said made sense. But Spencer wasn't willing to ignore his suspicions. "You say there have been others from Zeiss watching Miss Austin?"

"Yeah. For about a week now. Ever since she started talking to the D.A."

"A week?" Bailey set her towel on the island and circled around to stand beside Spencer. He didn't think it was the cool air or the shower that made her so pale. "You've been following me that long? In a black car?"

Max glanced at her in confusion. "I drive a pickup."

She glanced up, worried. "Spence? The watch?"

"I know." It had been mailed during the same week-long time frame. Spencer pulled out his business card and handed it to Duncan. "I want to know the names of every man assigned to her detail, with photo IDs and license numbers for personal vehicles as well as company cars. If you've got activity logs on those days she was being watched, I want those, too. You can email them to my computer at work."

"I'll have to ask my supervisor."

"No, you'll do it. Or I'll call Jackson Mayweather and tell him what a piss-poor job your team has done thus far. Bailey's received threats and she's been followed. Either your company hasn't been sharp enough to recognize the danger, or you're the ones spooking her."

Duncan unzipped his parka and held it open so Spencer could see him pull out his cell phone. "Sorry, ma'am. We'll make this right."

With a nod, Spencer pulled the Sig Sauer from his belt and handed it back. "Make sure you keep the safety on that gun when you're around Miss Austin."

Duncan growled a response. "I know how to do my damn job."

"Well, you'd better start doing it better than you have been." He slipped his hand beneath Bailey's elbow while Duncan made his call. "Can I talk to you?" he whispered, pulling her out into the hallway.

Spencer released Bailey and turned to face her while she closed the door behind them.

"Do you really think Mr. Zeiss's security team have been in the cars I thought were following me?"

Pulling back his coat and jacket, Spencer propped his hands at his waist and shrugged. "It's a possibility. I'll look into it more when I get to the precinct office."

"What if The Cleaner is blackmailing one of them? Or paid one of their staff a lot of money to betray me?" She curled her toes into the beige carpet and hugged her arms around her middle, clearly unsettled by the potential threat. "You said that's how she works, isn't it?"

"Yeah." Spencer couldn't keep looking at the hopeful trust in those blue eyes without feeling the need to pull her into his arms and make promises he couldn't keep. He turned his face to the ceiling and exhaled a deep breath before zeroing in on the loose tendrils of hair that clung to her cheeks and forehead. Still damp from the shower, her hair was a darker shade of wheat than its usual color, and added to Bailey's touchably soft and vulnerable look.

Damn his eye for detail.

It had to be fatigue that weakened his will like this. He took another deep breath to ease the raw need inside, and forced himself to look her straight in the eye. "I'll check out Zeiss backwards and forwards—make sure none of the employees have done something that can be used against them. I'll also run their bank accounts."

"I know you'll find The Cleaner."

"Let's just hope it's before she finds you." Spencer groaned at how that must sound. "I won't stop looking until I have her in my sights."

"I believe you. You're a mess," she gently teased, changing the subject. She reached up to straighten his collar while he was trying to be tough and professional and get through what he needed to say. She fastened the top two buttons of his shirt and adjusted the knot of his day-old tie, her fingers lightly brushing across his chest and neck. Nerve endings danced beneath his skin, chasing every firm, yet delicate touch. Spencer wasn't even strong enough to back away when she cupped the side of his jaw and rubbed her fingertips against the beard stubble there. "Looks like you've had a long night. Do you want some coffee? Breakfast?"

"No." He shouldn't want this, either.

"What are you doing here?" she asked, stroking her fingers along his jaw, as if she could feel the tension there.

He nodded toward the door. "Kincaid looked like he was breaking into the building. You're sure you trust him?"

"Yes. I've known him for a couple of years. His supervisor has worked for Jackson's company since I was a teenager. They provide security for Mother and Jackson's house, or when visiting dignitaries fly into town to do business with Jackson. I'm sure they'll be at the Ball on Saturday." Her fingers stopped their sensuous petting and she dropped her hands back to the middle of his chest. "I meant, why are you here in the first place? Or should I say the last place? Have you been watching over me, all night?"

He couldn't answer that. It would mean admitting more than he should. Still, his hands weren't getting the message from his brain, and they came up to settle over hers. "Why wouldn't your stepfather tell you he was assigning men to keep an eye on you?"

"Maybe he didn't want to infringe on my quest for independence. More likely, he didn't want to alarm my mother. She isn't dealing well with the risk I'm taking."

"*She* can't deal with it? You're the one who was assaulted."

"She doesn't understand my need to…fight back." Bailey pulled away and shoved her fingers through her hair, leaving a rumpled mess in their wake. "I think she wants it to all just go away so that she doesn't have to worry about me anymore. So she doesn't have to worry about anything but her parties and giving Jackson a beautiful home. Try to find some sympathy for her, Spencer. She's not a strong person."

"She leaked the threats you received to the press."

"I saw the news last night. Mother called to say Vanessa Owen had spoken to her." She shivered visibly before hugging her arms around herself again. "Vanessa told my mother it would be good PR for the Christmas Ball to mention my name."

That stupid ball. Such a public event. Although The Cleaner liked to work in the shadows, and catch her victims when they were vulnerable and alone, he still didn't like the idea of such a bright spotlight being focused on Bailey. Even if Zeiss Security proved to be a topnotch protection service, there'd be too many people to watch, too many opportunities to lose track of the D.A.'s star witness, too many ways she could get hurt.

"Are your parents going to make sure someone's with you around the clock?"

"I suppose."

"They better. Because I can't be here for you."

Her cheeks blanched to an unnatural shade of pale at his sharp tone. "But you were here all night..." Then she smiled, misunderstanding the meaning of his words. "That's okay. Do you work today? Will you have a chance to sleep?"

The emotions bubbled up, and his voice grew harsh as he tried to control them. "I'm talking long-term, Bailey. I want you to be safe. That's my top priority right now. I'll solve the damn case. But I can't be your bodyguard."

"I didn't ask—"

"If that bruiser loses track of you, or locks himself out again, and you're in trouble, remember the lesson I gave you. Nose, throat, gut and groin." Spencer caught her hands and pulled them to his face, neck and stomach. They lingered at his waist, then slid beneath his coat and jacket to his flanks. Her brave touch humbled him, branded him. "You're not like your mother. You're strong. You can take care of yourself."

"I understand. I'm responsible for my own safety. I'll talk to Jackson again. I'll make sure the security team introduces themselves to me so there are no more misunderstandings." Her eyes grew bright with tears she tried to blink away. "Thank you, anyway, for...being there for me when I needed you. I won't bother you again."

"That's not what I meant." His fingers locked on to her wrists, keeping her hands from pulling away. "If you need a cop, of course, I'll be here for you. You can always call. I just can't—"

"It's okay." She shushed him as one of the tears spilled over onto her cheek. "I know I'm an inconvenience. You have important work to do. I'm not the type of woman you need. You have a life of your own. Whatever the reason is, I can sense you don't want things to get personal between us. Even though..."

She didn't have to finish the sentence. It had been like this between them from day one. They were meant to be. But they couldn't be. The timing had never been right. He'd been grieving Ellen. She'd been engaged. Completing the task force's work was his sole mission. She needed a patience and sensitivity to recover from the rape he couldn't provide. And the situation now was as far from right as it could get.

Another tear left a shiny trail across her cheek and Spencer moved his thumb there to wipe it away from her cool skin. "I'm sorry." He tunneled his fingers into the damp silk of her hair and framed her head in his hands, tilting her face up to his as he drifted closer. "Work and relationships don't mix well for me. I've lost so much and you need more than I can give. You're something special, and I'm tempted, but..."

Her tears shimmered against the shadows of pain in her eyes, and a tight knot twisted deep in his gut at knowing he was any part of the hurt she felt. Spencer pressed a kiss to her forehead and lingered there, committing to memory the softness of her skin, the sunny warm scent of her hair, the sheer perfection of her brave spirit and gentle, compassionate soul.

"Thank you for understanding."

And when she should have nodded her head, when he should have pulled away, Bailey stretched up to kiss the corner of his mouth and whispered, "Thank *you*. For everything."

Ah, hell. She had a beautiful *woman's* mouth—as soft and sleek and sexy as the rest of her. Spencer felt the strain in his muscles, all the way down to his toes, as he fought the urge to move his lips over hers. He hovered. She waited. He wanted. Her breathy sigh was a tickle of warmth against his skin.

Spencer lost the battle and closed his mouth over hers. His fingertips tightened against her scalp. Hers dug into the sides of his waist. The tips of her breasts beaded against his chest as she leaned into the kiss, sending shards of longing south of his belt buckle and deeper inside. He stroked his tongue over the supple seam of her lips and they parted for him. With a stuttering hum of surrender she slid her tongue against his, tasting him as he plundered her mouth.

He pressed a kiss to the tip of her nose, to the corner of each eye where he sipped away the salty residue of her tears. When her arms slid around his waist and her sweet curves molded to his harder frame, he claimed her mouth again. He crowded his hips and thighs into hers, wanting to feel every exquisite inch of her against his body.

He was hungry for this woman, starving. She was holding on with both fists, giving everything he asked for, demanding he hold nothing back.

The kiss should have released the tension inside him, but it only coiled tighter and tighter.

Maybe that was the lesson to be learned from giving in to this kiss. What his heart and body wanted didn't matter.

Bailey Austin mattered.

And he couldn't do this *and* be the man she needed him to be.

It took all the strength he possessed to tear his mouth from hers and ease the tangle of his fingers in her hair. She leaned back against the wall, pulling her arms from his waist and resting them against the rapid rise and fall of his chest. Her deep breaths matched his own and the stunned look in her eyes matched what he was feeling inside.

"I haven't…," she began. Then her fingers curled around his tie as if she was reluctant to pull away entirely.

Spencer rested his forehead against hers and looked down to meet her upturned gaze. "You haven't what?"

"I haven't kissed a man since…before…" The rape. Ah, hell. He'd come on like a crazy man, practically driving her against the wall. He could have hurt her, scared her, reminded her— She tugged on his tie, as if reading his mind and reprimanding him for his regrets. "I haven't thought about anyone that way until you. I've never been so ready for a man to kiss me."

There were words to say—*thank-you's* and *you deserve better* and *I've been waiting for that kiss, too.*

But Spencer said none of those things. He thought of Ellen Vartran and just how much he could lose. He imagined Bailey dying in his arms, making promises she could never hope to keep.

He stroked her swollen lips with the pad of his thumb.

Walk away. Now.

Or he never would.

He took a step back, and retreated a lot farther inside. "You'll be fine. My people are going to track down the watch and whoever took those photos of you. I'll verify each of the men your stepfather has watching you. We'll get The Cleaner. You'll be just fine. I promise."

Bailey's eyes widened, then shuttered. She'd given him the finest compliment a man could ask for and he'd answered as if he were making a report to the chief. She pulled her hands from his tie, breaking their last contact. "I'll see you at the courthouse on Monday."

"Goodbye, B. Lock the door behind you."
She nodded and reached behind her to turn
the door knob and slip back inside. "Goodbye."

Chapter Eight

"Stop that." She swatted Brian's hand away when he reached down to rub the raw skin beneath the ankle bracelet that allowed KCPD to keep track of his movements.

"Here." Sitting on the edge of the bed, the woman dabbed a cotton ball soaked with hydrogen peroxide against the wounds where he'd scratched it. His breath hissed as she pushed aside his pajama pant leg to cleanse the self-inflicted wounds. "Poor thing," she sympathized, glancing at the clock on the bedside table as she reached for the ointment. Her colleague had better call soon. The police weren't the only ones with the ability to monitor their prey. She smiled as she straightened and opened the tube. "It must sting."

His hands fisted in the covers as he fought to control his illness. "I want it off. Now."

"You can't do that, darling." She rubbed the soothing gel beneath the ring on his leg.

"We have to show the judge how well you're cooperating with his mandate. You must be patient if we're going to win this case."

"At least if I go to prison I won't have to wear this damn thing anymore."

There he'd be living with mice and bugs and most likely a cell mate, with a stainless-steel toilet right there near the cot where he'd sleep. Brian couldn't survive a situation like that with his obsessive-compulsive disorder.

But she wasn't worried. "You aren't going to prison." He belonged in this hotel's penthouse suite with her, even if there was a black-and-white police car parked on the street below them. "Soon, everything will be taken care of."

His deep blue eyes demanded she see reason. "If Bailey Austin testifies—"

"She won't." *She* had always been the voice of reason in this relationship. He was the brilliant designer, the innovative business tycoon with a vision for restoring this city to its architectural splendor. Let him be the castle-builder whom so many people admired. She was the clever workhorse who did the unpleasant jobs, who smoothed over the rough patches of an illustrious career, who loved him despite his mood swings and obsessions. She wiped her fingers on a towel before gently touching his lips. "I promised I'd take care of you. And I always will."

He grabbed her wrist and pulled her hand from his mouth. "I am not some babe to be taken care of."

He swiped the towel from her hand and wiped his lips.

No. He was certainly a man. A great man in her eyes. Their relationship had to remain secret, but for years—longer than anyone might suspect—it had remained strong. They shared a stormy history of love and hate and lots of taking. They both had benefitted from this affair. But no one had ever needed her the way this man did. And for that need, for him, she would do anything.

The telephone rang and she got up, tying her robe securely around her waist. "There's the call I'm waiting for." She pointed a warning finger at him as he swung his feet to the floor. "Try not to scratch." When she reached the desk in the adjoining office, she picked up the phone. "Yes?"

"That red-haired cop—Montgomery—he was at her place again."

"I see." She kept her voice pleasant, and her smile in place so as not to alarm Brian. She'd just gotten him settled down. He'd surveyed his newest warehouse renovation project, and signed all the office papers and checks for the day. It was her time now. The time when he'd show just how much he still loved her, and why all her hard work on his behalf was worth it. "And now?"

"He drove off. He didn't look happy. Neither did she."

Good. Distance between Bailey Austin and the crusading detective would work to her advantage. The woman crossed her arms beneath her breasts and turned away. "Where is Bailey now?"

"Still in her apartment. You don't need me to keep doing this, do you? Spying on her?" Her colleague was wavering, questioning her instructions. "I mean, the trial starts in three days. If you haven't scared her off yet, then you're not going to. Maybe she's got more backbone than you think, and your plan won't work."

Her plans always worked. "Not only will you keep eyes on her and report anything you find out, you will take the next step. This afternoon, I think."

"I don't know. This doesn't feel right."

Now this just wouldn't do. Her colleagues could be easily replaced—but timing was crucial, and this one was in the perfect position to carry out her orders. Recruiting someone new would take time Brian didn't have. "Would you rather I leak the name of the strip club where you worked to the tabloids? Let's see, that particular establishment had connections to organized crime, didn't it? Wouldn't that make a juicy story on the evening news?" She paused to let the seriousness of the threat set in. "I have several reporters' numbers on speed dial."

"That would cost me my job and my license."

"And?" The long pause at the other end of the line meant cooperation was now guaranteed. Oh, how it paid to know other people's secrets.

"What do you need me to do?"

THE WIND WHIPPED across the hilltop at Mt. Washington Cemetery, stinging his cheeks and ruffling his hair, but Spencer didn't feel it.

The yellow rose he'd laid on the ground in front of the red marble marker had blown across the snow and caught in one of the foot prints he'd made when he'd dug down to uncover Ellen Vartran's grave. Twenty-seven years. Not nearly a long enough life. Only one year older than Bailey Austin.

He couldn't bury someone else at so young an age.

He couldn't lose another... Spencer couldn't bring himself to even think the word *love*. It just wasn't a part of his vocabulary anymore.

So why did he kiss Bailey?

Because he hadn't been thinking. He'd only been feeling.

That was a mistake he could never repeat. Or else he'd end up here on another dreary day with another flower.

Alive was the only outcome he wanted for Bailey Austin. The best way to ensure that was to keep a clear head, track down and erase The Cleaner and finish Brian Elliott's trial.

Love wasn't anywhere in that picture.

Okay, so maybe he was feeling the wintry chill a little. Inside, where a wool coat and knitted scarf didn't do him any good.

"Why'd you do it, El?" Spencer shoved his hands deep into the pockets of his coat, still wondering how that last night at the safe house had gone so wrong. Why hadn't he seen her looking for a way out of testifying against the men her brother had worked for? A better cop would have seen the darting looks, would have noticed his phone sitting on top of his clothes instead of inside the pocket of his jeans where he'd dropped them on the way into the shower with her. She hadn't trusted him enough to keep her safe, and she'd been right. He'd been focused on her, on them— he hadn't been paying close enough attention. "Why'd you make that phone call?"

His answer was the sound of an engine shifting into 4-wheel drive. Spencer turned his face into the north wind to see Nick Fensom's Jeep slowly climbing the hairpin turns and pulling to a stop on the road behind his Suburban. Nick had Annie with him, and the two were arguing about something until Nick leaned across the seat and kissed her. With a smile and a shake of her head, she nudged him toward the door and gave Spencer a small wave.

Spencer nodded in return as Nick left the motor running and climbed out. He tightened the gray scarf around his neck and clapped his gloved hands together against the cold. "Thought I'd find you here. Annie's worried you'll get frostbite. She says I need to talk you into coming over to the new house tonight for some takeout and friendly company."

"You just want to put me to work painting the new kitchen." This teasing give and take had always been easy with Nick. Sometimes, they were the only conversations he had all day that had nothing to do with work.

"Isn't that part of the best man's responsibilities? Helping his buddy remodel the old house the bride and groom are going to be moving into?"

Spencer glanced down at his partner's wise-ass expression. "That's what your brothers and sisters and contractor father are far. All I have to do is show up with the ring. And make sure you show up at the wedding."

Nick grinned and looked toward his Jeep. "Nothing's keeping me from spending the rest of my life with that woman."

"Good. We all chipped in so Annie would get you out of our hair."

Nick's laugh echoed off the trees surrounding the cemetery, and Spencer felt the constriction in his chest easing a little bit.

When the laughter stopped, the two men stood in silence for several seconds, paying their respects and simply being. But the reprieve couldn't last. "You know, Bailey Austin and Ellen Vartran aren't the same person."

Spencer stood half a head taller than Nick, was a better shot and had seniority over him. But the stocky, streetwise detective didn't back away from anything.

Even forbidden topics between friends.

"Stay out of my love life," Spencer warned.

A warning, which Nick duly ignored. "You don't have a love life, buddy." Even a well-practiced glare couldn't deter him. "Are you still not over Ellen? Is that what's holding you back?"

"Whatever Ellen and I had was brief and fiery and done. It was a younger man's love."

"Oh, yeah, because you are so over the hill at thirty-six."

Inhaling a deep breath that chilled his lungs and cleared his head, Spencer tried to explain. "Maybe it's the guilt you never get over. She used my phone that night in the safe house. Called her brother while I was in the shower, then joined me. Either she was distracting me from seeing the outgoing call or she was saying goodbye. When I came back the next morning, the safe house was already under attack. Her brother and the guard were dead. She was bleeding out." He stared at the rose carved beside Ellen's name. "I screwed up."

"As I recall, you got shot trying to save her—and you took out one of the hit men. KCPD rounded up the rest of the hit squad and Dwight Powers put them away."

"But it took us a lot longer to bring down

the rest of the organization. Ellen died and I blew our investigation."

"Bailey will testify." Nick said it like he believed it. Like there was no way she could be intimidated into changing her mind. Like she couldn't be harmed or killed. "Even if you screw up whatever you two should have going, she's still going to take down Brian Elliott for us. I can feel it in my gut. She's good for this."

As much as he trusted Nick's instincts about people, Spencer nodded toward the gravestone. "Even your gut can't guarantee that."

Nick propped his hands at his waist and challenged Spencer. "So what are you going to do about it?"

Spencer's logical brain warred with the rusty armor guarding his heart. But he knew where his strength lay. "You got a report for me?"

Nick muttered a curse before pulling a notepad from inside his leather jacket and flipping it open. "I looked into Zeiss Security. Zeiss is retired German military and his employees are all bonded and look legit. I left Sarge doing her computer magic at the office—she'll let us know if any of her in-depth research pops up anything suspicious."

"What's their connection to Bailey?"

"Zeiss subcontracts with Gallagher Security Systems and does most of the bodyguard and security work for GSS. They've been providing service for the Mayweathers for at least ten years."

"So they check out. What about Max Duncan?"

"Former Army—did most of his stint as an MP at Fort Leonard Wood." Nick snapped his notepad shut and put it away. "He's not your delivery man. I showed Duncan's picture to some of the other residents in Bailey's building. No one recognized him."

"I thought Corie Rudolf might be lying. She was just trying to score points with me. Like she's my type."

"Your type is a little classier. A little taller, a little blonder."

"Nick—"

"Why can't you just admit Bailey means something to you? I've never known you to lie to me, Spence. Don't lie to yourself, either." Nick puffed up like a fierce banty rooster beside him, daring him to deny the truth. "From the night we answered that rape call outside the Fairy Tale Bridal Shop, and you saw that the victim was Bailey Austin, this case has been personal for you."

"Chief Taylor put me in charge of this task force. I'm not going to blow the D.A.'s case or our investigation. I'm not going to let Elliott get away with rape or The Cleaner get away with murder." It was a valiant, solid argument.

But Nick wasn't buying it. "Remember which of us is the more stubborn partner."

"I thought you claimed to be the better-lookin' one."

Nick grinned. "That, too." But he quickly got serious. "It's okay to be happy, Spence. You saw what Annie and I could have long before I did." He reached over and squeezed Spencer's shoulder before giving it a smack and pulling away. "I'm trying to return the favor."

Spencer tucked his chin against the wind and pointed toward Ellen's marker. Damn it if Nick didn't make sense. Or was he only wanting him to make sense? "What if it happens again? I can't go through this twice."

"You didn't have me for a partner last time."

Spencer arched an eyebrow. "*That's* the argument you're going with?"

"You know I've got your back. Look, I don't know a more thorough cop than you. Don't know one who's smarter. You set 'em up and I finish the fight. Together, we get the job done. That's always worked for us." Nick patted Spencer's shoulder and started up the hill. "Come on. I'm freezing my yum-yums off out here."

"Tracking Bailey might be the best way to get a lead on The Cleaner," Spencer pondered out loud. If the stalker was targeting anyone but Bailey, that'd be the logical step he'd take.

"Told you you were the smart one." Nick had reached the side of the road. "Are you coming with us or heading back to Bailey's?"

As he worked out the viable scenarios, Spencer followed Nick's path through the snow. "I don't know yet."

Nick opened his door and a wave of warm air rushed out. "Just give me a call when you need that backup."

Spencer waited in his SUV behind Nick and Annie at the cemetery gate. When the light changed, Nick pulled out to the right.

Spencer turned left.

"I'M SURE SHOPPING isn't your favorite thing, Max." Bailey heard herself apologizing for the second time as they stepped off the tall curb and hurried across the street with the rest of the crowd on Kansas City's Country Club Plaza.

"Not a problem, Miss Austin." He took her elbow and helped her over the next curb, pausing to get his bearings at the five-way intersection. "You said it's up this way?"

She pointed to the tall sign outlined with white lights. "It's a couple of storefronts beyond the coffee shop."

He hurried her past a volunteer ringing a bell in front of a model train store. "I wish we could have parked closer. I don't like being out in the open like this."

Bailey gestured to the bumper-to-bumper cars lining the sidewalks. "Your only other option was to drop me off and find a parking space. And I know you didn't want to leave me alone."

"No," he agreed, pulling her into step beside him again. "Mr. Zeiss said I was to stay with you until my replacement comes this evening. And I sure as hell don't want that detective friend of yours breathing down my neck again."

"No. We certainly don't want that."

Thoughts of Spencer Montgomery made her steps stutter, and Max automatically shortened his stride to stay beside her.

She thought she'd been happily content, working around her apartment today, baking cookies and wrapping more presents. But when Max had reminded her that she needed to get down to the Plaza, and he'd rather do that while there was still some daylight out, Bailey realized she'd been hiding out. Maybe even feeling sorry for herself.

Wasn't that the same thing as being a prisoner? She wouldn't let difficult circumstances make her a victim again. Maybe Spencer hadn't stayed. She understood that his work was more important than babysitting her until Monday.

But that kiss this morning had felt so right that she thought he was feeling the same irresistible draw she was. She didn't have a crush on the man. It wasn't gratitude. It was a bone-deep attraction to his strength, his intelligence, that protective nature, his unquestionable code of honor. And it had meant so much more.

That desperate, feverish embrace against the hallway wall was the first thing in a long time that she'd been sure of. She wasn't a poor little rich girl who needed to be taken care of. She wasn't a victim. She was a woman—real, strong, necessary.

It was as if all the jumbled pieces of her life this past year had finally fallen into place. Holding Spencer, tasting him, absorbing his strength—knowing he wanted her gave her confidence, made her feel stronger.

But the kiss had been a mistake.

Spencer didn't want her in that way. There was some mutual lust there—she wasn't so naive to pretend there wasn't—but it hadn't meant the same thing to him. He'd just gotten caught up in the moment and had been too exhausted to fight it. All he really wanted was a witness to close his case.

The crushing blow to her heart had nearly sent her to bed. And that's when Bailey knew she had to get out of her well-appointed prison and do something with her day—do something with her life. She wouldn't sit there and pine over a man who'd made it clear he didn't want to want her.

It might not be much, but she could help her mother with the Christmas Ball. She could show up, be a gracious hostess and help raise lots of money for a good cause. She could reassure her mother's fractured nerves that her daughter was safe and happy and okay. Well, two of the three. Maybe then her mother wouldn't worry quite so much when Bailey took the witness stand.

Alleviating her mother's fears. That was something useful she could do.

So she'd put on warm slacks, a sweater and

boots, convinced Max that she had only one stop to make at the Plaza shops and braved the holiday crowds to pick up her dress for tomorrow night.

It was nice to have Max's muscle clear a space for her through the tourists lined up to watch the animated window displays and the shoppers hurrying up and down the wide sidewalks to get to their next destination. Max didn't have to touch anyone to literally clear a path. But something about the big shoulders and unsmiling face made people walk a wide berth around him, and since she was connected to him by his hand on her elbow, they walked a wide berth around her, as well.

Until the coffee shop door swung open and Corie Rudolf dashed out. "Bailey?"

"Corie?"

"Look out." They would have collided with each other if Max hadn't grabbed the door and pulled Bailey to a stop. "Everybody okay?" he asked, pushing the door closed and pulling Bailey into the vestibule in front of the shop.

Corie beamed a smile up at Max. "No harm done."

But the shorter woman was juggling her purse, her cell phone and a tall cup of coffee. Bailey reached out to take the coffee for a moment before Corie spilled it down the front of her short coat and long, cream-colored scarf. "Oops. Not in the clear yet."

"Thanks." Corie tucked her phone into her purse and straightened the matching cream knit cap she wore before taking her coffee back. "That was a close one."

"What are you doing here?" Bailey asked.

Max eyed the couple coming out of the coffee shop while Corie dodged the passersby on the sidewalk. "My date canceled on me. I remembered you said you were coming down to the Plaza, and I thought we could grab a coffee or maybe take in a movie?" She patted the side of her purse where she'd tucked her cell. "I was just calling your number to see if I could track you down in this crowd."

Bailey glanced up at her bodyguard, and he was already shaking his head. "The movie's out," she explained to Corie. "We were on our way to the formal shop. You're welcome to join us if you'd like."

"Sure. Maybe I could try on one of those fancy dresses, too." A gap formed in the stream of pedestrians on the sidewalk as the lights at the intersection changed. Corie backed up and started walking with them. She pointed to her tiny compact car as they approached. "I'm parked right here. Maybe I'd better put my coffee inside."

Bailey agreed. "I'm sure the store manager won't want that around his merchandise."

"I'm glad I found you." Whatever awkwardness Corie had displayed earlier was gone as she quickened her pace to get a few steps ahead. She looked around Bailey to Max. "I owe you an apology. I hope I didn't get you into trouble with Detective Montgomery. I'm not very good with faces. But I do remember backsides, and yours..."

"Corie," Bailey chided her with a smile. The woman was shameless.

All was forgiven, apparently, because Max grinned, flattered. "Mine's better, right?"

Corie pulled out her keys to press the remote. "Let's just say I certainly would have remembered—"

Bailey saw a flash of light beneath the hood of the car an instant before Corie flew into the air and the deafening shock wave of the exploding car knocked Bailey to the ground.

Fiery embers took a bite out of her cheek and arm. Her head rang with the concussive noise. Glass shattered and fell down like snow. The ball of fire burning in the street hurt her eyes and she looked away to see people running away, mouths open, screaming without making a sound.

She turned her head the other direction to see Max rolling on the sidewalk, clutching his leg. He had scrape marks along the sleeve of his coat and a hole at the elbow where the insulated material had been completely torn away.

Max was saying something to her, pointing toward the street. He repeated himself, maybe shouting this time because she could hear his words like a muffled whisper through the fog of her brain. "Are you okay? Is she okay?"

Bailey nodded. Other than the ringing in her ears and the burning on her cheek and wrist, she couldn't feel any broken bones. Bracing her hands against the concrete, she pushed herself to a sitting position. She touched her fingers to her aching cheek and came away with blood on her glove. Her coat was grimy and torn, with more red drops staining the chest and sleeve. "I'm okay," she repeated with more force, wondering if Max could hear her. "I'm okay."

"What about Blondie?" She heard Max again, more clearly this time, and turned her head.

"Corie!"

The decorative shrubs near Corie's shell of

a car were burning. Corie lay at the base of the hedge, her chest panting with fast shallow breaths. There was blood in her ear, at the corner of her mouth. Her cream-colored scarf and hat were both turning red with the blood.

"Oh, my God." Heedless of the aches and bruises of her own body, Bailey crawled across the ice-cold sidewalk to her friend. "Corie?"

She dragged her friend's body away from the fire, apologizing for every shriek of pain she caused. When the heat from the burning wreckage felt less intense, Bailey unwound her scarf and wadded it up to place it beneath Corie's neck. But then what? She needed to help, but didn't know where to start. The head wound? The glazed eyes? The twisted shard of metal in her chest?

"Oh, Corie, I'm sorry." Memories of broken watches and complicated devices of her own imagination filled her head. Annie Hermann had warned her of the possibility of a bomb—that the threats against her could have very real consequences. But Bailey hadn't completely understood—Spencer had been right—she had no idea of the scope of the danger she was facing, no idea that anyone else could get hurt. Because of her. Her fault.

Suddenly, Bailey couldn't catch her breath. Someone else was controlling her life again. Her eyes filled with tears at the enormity of what was happening here. Corie wasn't the only one hurt. Max was, too. Maybe others. Someone else had a vicious, violent power over her. Over them all. She was helpless. Useless. Afraid.

"Stop it!" Corie's unfocused eyes opened at her shout.

"You're strong. You can take care of yourself."

Spencer's encouraging words, even as he'd been saying goodbye, echoed through her. Someone did believe in her. Someone thought she was strong enough to get through adversity.

She *was* strong enough. Bailey swiped the tears from her eyes and urged her shivering friend to look at her. "Corie?" She untied her coat and eased it off over the cut on her wrist. She could hear sirens in the distance now, horns honking, people shouting. "Corie? Can you hear me?" Bailey spread her coat over her friend, carefully avoiding the shrapnel on the left side of her chest. Then she scooped up Corie's hand. There was no answering response, but she squeezed it anyway. "I need to go check on Max. Okay, sweetie? Don't close your eyes."

The wintry air seeping into her skin, and floating debris landing on her clothes barely registered. There was so much blood on the sidewalk beneath Corie. Her pupils were dilated, her skin so pale.

"KCPD! Clear the area. Get back! Bailey?" There was one voice in the crowd, shouting above the others—more intense, more authoritative than any other.

Spencer.

"Spence!" Bailey lurched to her feet. She spotted the red hair first.

"B!" He tucked his badge into his pocket as he pushed through the crowd. His long coat billowed out when he opened his arms and Bailey threw herself against his chest. His arms cinched around her, lifting her onto her toes as he pressed a kiss to her temple and surrounded her with his warmth and strength. "Are you okay?"

"I thought you weren't coming back." She locked her arms around him and turned her face into his neck, inhaling his clean, familiar scent. "Thank God, you did."

"Are you hurt?" There was another quick kiss before he set her down and framed her face between his hands. Those cool gray eyes scowled like fury as they took in the cut on her face. "Ah, hell." With his sharp gaze darting from one compass point to the next, he released her entirely and shrugged out of his coat. He swung it over her shoulders and buttoned it together at her neck. "You're freezing."

The weight and warmth was pure comfort, but Bailey knew she wasn't the one who needed his attention. "I'm okay. Max's leg is broken and Corie…" Clutching his coat around her, she pushed away and dropped to her knees beside her friend. "Her car exploded. Just as we were walking past. We have to help her."

Spencer peeled off one glove and knelt beside Bailey to check Corie's neck for a pulse. He wrapped an arm around Bailey's shoulders. "I don't know, sweetheart."

"I have to call for help."

"Already done." He glanced up and Bailey followed his gaze to the cars that had rear-ended each other on the street, to the drivers on their cell phones. To the curious onlookers in the windows of the shops across the street, and on the sidewalk below—so many of them on their phones or taking pictures. There were red and blue flashing lights farther away, uniformed cops clearing traffic to get a fire engine to the scene.

"Bailey Austin?" She heard whispers from the crowd. "Is that Bailey Austin?"

She ignored the curious pointing fingers and flashing telephones and looked down to her friend. "Her eyes are closed again. We have to help her."

"I don't think we can." She felt Spencer's hands pinching around her shoulders, pulling her to her feet. "I need to get you out of here."

"But Corie—"

"I'll stay with her," Max volunteered, sliding over on his hip and uninjured arm. "My knee's shattered. I'm not going anywhere." He looked up at Bailey, then to Spencer. "Take care of her."

"I'm so sorry," Bailey repeated over and over to her fallen friends as Spencer dropped his arm behind her waist and turned her away.

"We have to go, B."

Bailey pushed against his hand and twisted from his grasp. "This is my fault. I have to help."

"Sweetheart, you need medical attention." He caught her hand and pulled her back beside him. "I need to get you out of here."

Bailey planted her feet and shoved against his chest. "Spencer, stop! I can help."

But he didn't budge. His hands were anchored to her shoulders again. "There are too many people. I can't control this crime scene. Someone just tried to kill you and they may try again." He hunched down to look her straight in the eye. "Do you want anyone else to get hurt?"

The harsh reminder drained the anger, the desperation, right out of her. She shook her head. "That was supposed to be me. They were after me."

He wrapped his arms around her, coat and all, and she burrowed against him. He walked her toward the parting crowd. "I know, B. I know."

That's when the first shot rang out.

Chapter Nine

"Get down!"

Spencer pulled Bailey to the ground and bent his chest over her as he pulled his gun and craned his neck to see where the shot had come from.

A second shot shattered the storefront window above their heads. Bailey screamed.

"Move!" he shouted to the curious onlookers still gathered around, trying to steal a picture or standing there in shock. "Get out of here!"

A third shot clipped the branch off a landscaping tree and he dragged Bailey into the snowbank, closer to the curb where the parked cars offered some protection. The gunfire was coming from a higher vantage point from someplace across the street.

"Go!" At last the people were running, saving themselves. He glanced back to see Max Duncan taking cover behind the dying fire of Corie Rudolf's shell of a car. He caught glimpses of uniformed officers hurrying in, guiding people to safety.

Spencer caught the eye of one uni and waved him over, but a shot chipped the bricks above his head and he was forced to duck behind a concrete pillar at the entrance to a nearby parking garage. If they couldn't get reinforcements to him, then they needed to go after the shooter. "Get someone on that roof! Now!"

With a nod, the young man pulled out his radio and darted back the way he'd come.

After the fifth shot, Bailey fisted her hands in Spencer's jacket and he glanced down to see the despair looking up from those deep blue eyes, asking if she was the cause of this chaos, too.

But she already knew the answer. He cupped his hand beside her undamaged cheek. "We need to make a run for it, sweetheart. Can you do that for me?"

He saw no other wounds than that bloody gash on her pale cheek and the cut at her wrist. She startled when a sixth shot blew out a string of lights on a nearby awning, dropping the bulbs to the pavement, where they exploded like mini ricochets off the concrete. Ellen's dark eyes were just a flash of memory.

Bailey was pulling him down to her, pulling herself up. Her blue eyes were clear. And she was nodding. "I can run."

The seventh shot meant an automatic weapon or more than one gun or magazine of bullets. The explosion had been a distraction. Using Bailey for target practice was the goal. If the bomb hadn't killed her, the sniper on top of the roof was here to finish the job.

The parking garage offered better protection than the open sidewalk. But twenty, twenty-five feet to the entrance? Or a closer leap over the divider wall to get inside? Either way, that was several feet of open ground, and his spare Kevlar was in the trunk of his car.

"What are we waiting for?" Bailey asked, pushing to sit up before he was ready for her to expose even the curls on top of her head.

He pushed her back into the snow, crazily aware of the warmth of her body buried beneath his, and shouted over his shoulder. "Duncan! You got eyes on the shooter?"

"Not yet. But he's on the roof of the Mercantile Building." The muscle man's every other word was a curse, but he had his gun at the ready and his aim fixed upward. "Go! Get her out of here. I'll lay down cover fire."

Shots eight and nine answered when Duncan fired his first round.

Time was precious, and that sidewalk was way too open for his liking. And he was all that stood between Bailey and the next bullet. "Ah, hell." Propping himself up on his elbows. Spencer holstered his gun and untucked his shirt from his belt, ripping at the buttons.

When he reached inside to tear apart the straps on his own vest, Bailey's hands were there to stop him. "Don't you dare. I don't want anyone else to get hurt."

"B—"

"If he shoots you, who'll take care of me? How will I get out of here and get to that trial?"

Of all the crazy times to have a logical, smarter-than-he-was thought…

Groaning, cursing, he grabbed her hand and pulled her to her feet. "You'll take care of yourself, damn it. Now, Duncan!"

With the rapid shots from Max's Sig Sauer keeping the shooter at bay for a few seconds, Spencer shielded his body around Bailey's and ran for the parking garage wall.

"Hold on!"

Bailey latched on tight when he dove over the wall. Another shot whizzed over their heads before they hit the concrete hard and rolled. Spencer twisted to take the brunt of the fall, but he was going to feel the impact in his hip and shoulder tomorrow.

Just as vividly as he felt Bailey's legs tangled between his now. Though they lurched to a stop against the wheel of a car and rebounded a few inches across the floor, her arms held on as though she never intended to let go. She was fighting to get through this. Fighting to live. Her cheek was cool against his, her hair was a citrusy balm that eased some of the concern out of him with each rapid breath.

"We're okay, sweetheart." He wound his arm behind her back, absorbing the aftershocks trembling through her body, keeping her close as he turned onto his side to get a glimpse over the top edge of the wall. Good. No direct sight line from the Mercantile's roof. He wound the other arm around her and kissed the silky hair at her temple. "We're okay, B."

She loosened her grip on his neck and framed his jaw between her hands. Even though she was nodding, her eyes were looking to him for reassurance. "Okay." She tugged on his face and pressed a sweet kiss against his lips. "Okay."

His entire body spasmed in an ill-timed response to those gentle lips pillowing against his. Her warm breath against his cold skin made him want to consume her as much as he wanted to comfort her. But he understood his priorities, even if the long thigh wedged precariously between both of his and the thundering response of his pulse tried to tell him something different.

But Bailey's eyes looked away before he could say something distancing and appropriate. "I don't hear any more shooting."

Do your job.

Exhaling a cloudy breath of air, Spencer pulled away, glad for the chilly temps and lack of a coat to keep his head clear. Keeping them both low to the floor, he helped Bailey sit up with her back against the divider wall. He knelt down beside her, quickly checking for any new injuries, batting away her hands as they tried to do the same for him.

"You're right." He nodded at the ongoing silence. Well, people were still shouting, horns were honking and sirens were blaring. But there was no gunfire.

He counted sixty seconds of silence before he risked peering over the top of the wall. No movement on the roof, no flash of a reflection that would indicate a weapon. "Duncan! Duncan, can you hear me? Report!"

"Max?" He let Bailey get up to her knees, but kept her beside him.

"I'm okay," the bodyguard finally answered. "Shooting's stopped. Lousy shot. Doesn't look like he hit anybody. Did your men get him?"

Spencer pulled his radio from his belt and called in. "This is Detective Spencer Montgomery. Senior officer on the scene. Did we get the shooter?" There was a long pause of static and chatter on the line. "Did we get him?"

The line cleared and Spencer got the answer he needed—but didn't want to hear. "Negative, sir," an officer answered. "I've got footprints in the snow up here, but there's no one but us."

"Shell casings?"

"Negative. We've got nothing. He must have gone down the fire escape and disappeared into the crowd."

All right. So The Cleaner or her latest thug had gotten away. She could have her victory. For now. But priorities shifted when the threat went underground. That meant moving on to canvassing the neighborhood. Taking care of injured people and a safe, orderly evacuation of this part of the city before anyone else got hurt. Although Spencer preferred to get his hands around the bastard's neck in an interrogation room, he knew what he had to do.

"Get a bus here ASAP. We've got a DB at the explosion site and a wounded man." The Plaza was a maze of pricey shops and entertainment venues with multiple entrances, several parking garages and crisscrossing streets. No way could they stop every person to search for a weapon. But they had to try. "Get Chief Taylor on this. Call it in to top brass. Deputy Commissioner Madigan is a friend of mine—my partner's uncle. Ask him free up any men we can spare. I want every vehicle stopped before it leaves the Plaza district. I want a patrol in every shop. I want eyes in the crowd. Call Pike Taylor and tell him we need K-9 units here. We need to find this shooter."

"Yes, sir."

Spencer put the radio back on his belt, made sure it was safe to stand, and helped Bailey to her feet. She was battered and bleeding. There was snow in her hair and a smear on his coat. But she was gorgeous. And alive. "You okay?"

"Not a hundred percent," she answered honestly. "But okay enough. You?"

"I'm okay." Bumps and bruises, frustration and nagging fears didn't count.

She could see his thoughts were distracting him as he leaned over the concrete divider and looked back toward the burning car and potential kill zone. Bailey peeked out, too. "No one else was hurt, were they?"

Spencer pulled her back inside the relative security of the parking garage and moved her behind this first row of cars toward the exit gate. He sealed his hand around hers and kept her beside him. "No one was supposed to get hurt."

Her fingers tightened around his. "How do you explain my dead friend?"

Spencer flipped his collar up against the cold. "With ten bullets, even a lousy shot would get lucky and hit somebody. Those shots were all aimed over our heads. Warning shots."

"To scare us?" Bailey stopped. "To scare me?"

"Did it work?" He turned and threaded his fingers through her tousled hair, gently freeing them from the wound on her cheek. He didn't want Bailey to be scared. Seeing her brave spirit cowed in any way bothered him as much as seeing her hurt. Nick had been right—he was lying to himself if he thought he didn't have feelings for this woman.

"Miss Austin?" Spencer pulled his gun and whirled around at the male voice behind him. "Whoa! I'm innocent!"

A young man, maybe twenty, with curling dark hair and a bright red Chiefs parka, flattened his back against the pillar at the front gate and raised his hands in surrender. "Take off your coat."

"What?"

"Take off your coat," Spencer repeated, keeping the business end of his gun pointed straight at the kid. "Are you carrying any weapons?"

"No, sir. No, officer." He unzipped the parka and dropped it at his feet, thrusting his hands back into the air and turning around, giving Spencer a better view of any hidden gun. "All I have is this."

"Spencer." He saw the green envelope in the kid's hand at the same time Bailey touched his arm, urging him to lower his weapon. "Where did you get that?"

Keeping a nervous eye on the man with the gun, the kid inched forward, holding the envelope out to Bailey. But Spencer snatched it from his hand before she could touch it. They both recognized the same green stationery that had come in the package with the watch. The young man hugged his arms around his middle, shivering in his baggy jeans. "A lady in the crowd said I should give it to Miss Austin. I know who you are from the newspapers, ma'am." He smiled at Bailey but frowned at Spencer. "Can I put my coat back on now?"

"Can you give me a description of that woman?" Spencer prompted.

Once he'd holstered his gun and nodded permission to bundle up again, the kid answered, "No. We were getting jostled around—my buddy and me—with all the people running away from the explosion. She slipped the card and a hundred-dollar bill in my hand and said not to look."

"What about your buddy—did he get a look?"

"I don't know. We got separated." The young man shrugged into his coat and zipped it up. "The lady said if I didn't turn around, there was another hundred in it for me." He brushed the dust and snow from his parka and shrugged. "I'm a college student. I didn't look."

A uniformed officer had arrived on the scene. Spencer raised his hand to tell the startled young man to relax, and to tell the officer to keep his service weapon holstered.

This kid was a witness, not a threat. "I need you to go over to that officer there and describe anything you can remember about the woman. Her height, what she smelled like, what she was wearing."

"Yes, sir."

"And I need those two bills."

"Oh, man," the kid whined. "I knew this was too good to be true. Do you know how much gas that'll put in my car?"

Bailey tilted her face up to him. "Do you think you can get trace off those bills?"

"Probably not. But I'm going to try."

Huddled inside his oversize coat, Bailey probably looked as nonthreatening as he looked like an armed menace. She took a couple of steps closer to the boy. "Give the police officer your name and address, and I'll write you a check for *three* hundred dollars."

The young man glanced from Bailey up to Spencer and back.

Spencer helped him decide. "We're not giving you a choice, son. Three hundred or nothing. I'd take the deal."

"Yes, sir." He quickly pulled the money from his pocket and handed it to Spencer who stowed it in a plastic evidence bag from his pocket while the kid walked out with the officer.

Once they were alone again, and Spencer had called Nick to alert the rest of the task force, Bailey nodded to the card he was holding in his gloved hand. "I believe that's for me."

As soon as he got to his SUV and a second evidence bag, he was putting it away. "Do you even need to open it?"

Fragile and feminine to look at, but made of pretty stern stuff. "Corie's dead, isn't she."

He knew she counted on him to be honest and up front with her, but he hated saying anything that would add to the sadness in her eyes. "I wasn't getting a pulse."

Spencer slipped his arm around her as he handed her the card. She leaned against him and slipped her thumb beneath the flap of the envelope. "Then let's see what that murdering witch has to say for herself."

I see you when you're sleeping.

I know when you're awake.

I can find you anytime, anywhere.

It's your choice—say Brian Elliott raped you...or live to see Christmas.

SPENCER WAS STILL on the phone. He sat at the big walnut desk in the alcove beneath the stairs leading to the second floor of his suburban condo, jotting notes and asking concise questions. When she'd gone into the kitchen to retrieve the scissors she'd spotted after dinner, he'd been pacing through the living room. As soon as they'd walked in to the modern condominium, with its tall windows, dark wood and gray walls, he'd locked the door, shown her where the bathroom and towels were, and picked up the phone.

She was guessing the man wasn't used to having company. And that her nightmarish afternoon on the Plaza had put almost all of Kansas City's finest on some kind of duty tonight.

Bailey hitched up the black KCPD sweatpants Spencer had lent her and padded across the polished wood floor in the white athletic socks she'd borrowed from him. The shower and clean clothes, even if the sweats were several sizes too large for her, had been a refreshing, comforting welcome after her trip through the E.R., a lengthy interview with Detective Nick Fensom and a quick meeting with her trauma counselor, Kate Kilpatrick.

She was fine. She was safe. She'd shared a heart-wrenching phone call with her mother and stepfather. Her mother had cried the entire time and Jackson had promised to give her a sedative and make sure she got a decent night's sleep.

Bailey sat on the black leather couch and curled her legs beneath her, trying to concentrate on cutting shapes out of the white paper she'd borrowed from Spencer's computer printer. She was doing her best not to eavesdrop on his investigation. But it was hard not to pick up on the gist of the conversations he'd had these past few hours.

He'd had several calls from his partner, Nick Fensom, talking *plan B* and *perimeter security*. Annie Hermann had called with results from the lab—no usable trace on the cash The Cleaner had paid the college student to deliver that last threat, but she was following up on several calls to and from Corie Rudolf's cell phone before she'd died. Someone named Pike Taylor and a police dog had reported on tracking the shooter from the roof of the Plaza Mercantile Building. But that trail had gone cold with time and snow and some type of chemical on the sidewalk.

Spencer could be talking to the deputy commissioner or Mitch Taylor or any of a hundred other police officers, lab techs and who knew what kind of experts right now.

And she…was cutting snowflakes.

Spencer leaned back in his leather desk chair, smoothing his hand over his damp red-gold hair. "No, Kate. Tell the press Miss

Austin isn't giving any interviews before the trial. And if I see any more photographs from today's attack on the television or in a newspaper or online, you can inform them that I'll be charging them with witness tampering."

Bailey unfolded her grade-school creations and carried them to the tall silk fern by the living room window. She'd already raided Spencer's desk for a box of colored paper clips that she'd hooked together and draped like garland through the fern's long leaves.

Although she could see the lights of the downtown skyline from the seventh-story window, Spencer lived far enough from the main highways and thoroughfares that the sky was nearly black when she looked outside. The moon wasn't even bright enough to pierce the low-hanging clouds or lighten her mood.

Still, she anchored the paper snowflakes to the clips, determined not to slip into one of those desperate funks that could be even more dangerous to her recovery than those anger episodes she sometimes had to deal with since the rape.

"It's close enough." Spencer rose from his chair to pace again. "The judge is already threatening to sequester the jury before the trial even starts. Endangering Bailey and jeopardizing the fairness of this trial sounds like tampering to me." She watched his reflection in the window, and saw when his attention shifted from the phone call to her. "I'd better let you get to bed. Is Sheriff Harrison in town with you? He's a good man. Thanks, Kate."

Spencer set the phone on the coffee table as he crossed the room to join her at the window. He scrubbed his hand over his jaw before splaying his fingers at the waist of his jeans. "What are you doing now?"

Bailey stood back from her handiwork. "Pretty pathetic, isn't it?"

"You're hanging paper clips on my fern."

"It's a Christmas tree." She caught the long sleeves of the sweatshirt she wore in her fists and hugged her arms around her waist. Right. Like that didn't sound lame.

"You've already fixed us an omelet and washed the dishes. My kitchen has never been that clean." Spencer propped his hip on the ledge of the window and sat back to face her. "I didn't bring you to my place to cure my Scrooge-ish spirit. I brought you here so I can keep you safe. Away from all that craziness out there today. This way I can keep an eye on you while I work on tracking down the shooter and who might have put that bomb together."

He'd missed a button on the collar of the striped oxford shirt he wore. Bailey curled her fingers into the soft cotton shirt, fighting the urge to button it for him. "I know you have to work. I don't begrudge you that for a minute. But there's nothing for me to do here except think. I don't have any clothes to unpack until Sergeant Murdock brings the suitcase from my place. I don't have a job with work I can bring home. I have to do something to stay busy." She spun away from the window, gesturing to both floors. "And you weren't kidding when you said you didn't celebrate Christmas. There's not a stitch of decoration or a present to be seen anywhere around here."

She heard him stand and felt his hands close around her shoulders. "B, you don't have to take care of me. I'm used to working late and fending for myself."

Bailey turned. "Maybe you don't need anything, but I…" She reached up and fastened the tiny button before smoothing the open placket of his shirt. "I need…to take care of you. I can do little jobs while you're working. I want to help."

He captured her hands as they moved

across the crisp material and pulled her to the couch to sit beside him. "You're not useless."

"You remember me saying that?" Bailey's cheeks flooded with heat and she pulled away. The man never forgot a detail, did he?

Spencer perched on the edge of the couch, taking her hands and rubbing them between his bigger, warmer ones. "You don't think putting Brian Elliott away in prison is the bravest, most helpful thing you can do? Think of all the women you're protecting by getting him off the streets. Think of families you're saving from heartbreak and tragedy."

He'd hunched down to her level and those handsome gray eyes were right there in front of her. The sincerity she read there was fiercely sweet. Bailey smiled her thanks, but pulled her fingers free to hold his in her lap. "I know that's important. And trust me, I'm not forgetting what a challenge it will be to talk about that night again in front of Brian and all those other people, strangers I don't even know, who'll be in that courtroom."

He waited patiently for her to continue, and Bailey discovered that having Spencer Montgomery focused solely on her—listening, watching, caring—could be as empowering as it was intimidating.

Her grasp tightened around his. "But the only reason I'm any help to you or the police department or Kansas City is because that man beat me until I was unconscious and did…unspeakable things to me."

"B—"

"No." She pulled away when he reached for her, trying to make things right, trying to take care of her and make the pain go away. She would have moved away, but his hand settled lightly on her knee, silently asking her to stay close and finish what she had to say. "What else do I have to offer the world, Spencer? When this trial is done, I don't want to be that poor little rich girl again. I want to do something meaningful with my life. I need to be something more than what I was…before. And if all I can do is wash your dishes and bring a lame little bit of Christmas into this sterile home, then that's what I'm going to do."

He studied her for several long seconds, taking in the butterfly bandage on her cheek, her vehement words, her frustration. Then his hand tightened around her knee and he leaned in to kiss her. His left hand tunneled into her hair to hold her at the nape and anchor her lips to his until she surrendered to his gentle persuasion and parted for him. She caught his jaw with her hand, holding on as he deepened the kiss.

It was tender, leisurely, giving, sweet. She tasted the coffee from dinner on his tongue and felt a languid heat curling inside her belly and seeping out into every extremity until she was far too warm for a winter's evening, and far too bewitched to recall the unsettling emotions that had left her feeling raw and second-rate just a few minutes earlier.

"I don't understand," she whispered on a husky voice when he finally broke away.

Spencer's fingers lingered in her hair and he rested his forehead against hers. His deep, uneven breaths made her think he'd gotten lost for a few moments in that kiss, too. But he was smiling when he straightened and looked into her eyes. "You're ambitious, Bailey Austin." His fingers stroked the hair at her nape. "As horrible as that night must have been for you—and as angry as it makes me to think a man would ever put his hands on you like that—I think the attack awakened a fighting spirit in you. You're no longer content to accept the status quo. You want to make your own decisions, make your own mistakes, create your own victories. You'll never settle for having them handed to you again."

A year's worth of therapy sessions with her counselor, and she'd never heard her internal struggle verbalized for her so perfectly.

"Yes."

Spencer understood. As twisted and complicated as her life had become, as volatile and bewildering as her emotions could be, he understood. She just wanted to be a normal woman again. Maybe for the first time in her life. With all his logic and acrimony and deductive genius, he got that.

No wonder she'd fallen in love with the man.

Even as the revelation blossomed in her heart and filled her with an anticipation and apprehension that were too new and unfamiliar to fully understand, he was pulling her to her feet and leading her across the living room to the foyer closet.

"I guess I have to ask you to be patient and not try to conquer all those battles tonight. Here." He pulled a box off the top shelf and handed it to her. "These are a few things I kept from my parents' estate." He lifted the lid to reveal a tray of glass ornaments, thinning silver garland and a pair of clumsily painted angels made out of popsicle sticks and cupcake wrappers—one red, one green.

Bailey lifted the green angel from its tissue wrapping and held it up. "Did you make these?"

"Yeah. A couple or thirty years ago." Spencer closed the box of decorations and carried it to the coffee table. "I think my mom kept everything I made in school."

"They're precious."

"I'm not leaving you alone to go get a real tree, but—" he pointed to the window where the silk plants are "—the ferns are all yours."

Laughing, she impulsively threw her arms around his neck and hugged him. "Who'd have that the stoic detective had a sentimental streak?"

"Don't let that get around the precinct, okay?" For a few moments, he hugged her back. Then his hands slipped to her waist and he was pushing some space between them. The stoic detective truly had returned. "I've got two more calls to make. We're trying to get some more background on Corie Rudolf. We dumped the numbers on her phone and discovered she'd made and received several calls from the same disposable cell number—almost all of them after the D.A. announced you'd be testifying at Elliott's trial. The last one came right before that bomb went off today."

Corie had been on the phone when she'd come out of the coffee shop. Maybe she hadn't been trying to call Bailey at all. Maybe her neighbor had followed her to the Plaza. "Do you think Corie was working for The Cleaner?"

"It's a possibility," Spencer admitted. "But not a fact yet. I need to run down a few more leads." He reached around her to pick up his phone. "Will transforming this bachelor pad into something more festive be meaningful enough work for now?"

Bailey nodded, sobered by the possible treachery of a friend who'd been murdered. "Thank you. You do your job. I'll be fine."

The rest of the evening passed by in relative silence between Bailey and Spencer. He worked until about midnight while she created a unique, silly display in the window that brought some childish fun and holiday colors to the otherwise austere condo. Bailey took her thoughts to bed with her and was sound asleep in the guest bedroom by the time Spencer came up the stairs.

Chapter Ten

It was 2:00 a.m. when Bailey rolled over in the dark, tangled in the covers of an unfamiliar bed, and the panic hit.

"Don't hurt me!" She fought against the tape that bound her wrists.

He was here.

"I told you not to look at me, you filthy witch!" Her captor pulled the hood over her face, plunging her into darkness. "You're like every other woman who doesn't know her place. I'm the man here." Her body jerked as he ripped her skirt off her hips. She screamed as he cut through her slip and pantyhose. The spicy, musky assault of his cologne burned into her memory as his weight crushed her into the mattress and plastic underneath her.

"Bailey?"

Lights flashed behind her eyelids. He was pouring something all over her, washing her

*body with a pungent liquid, inside and out.
"No!"*

*Her nightmare exploded in a blast of fire
and pain, throwing her to the ground. She
fought to escape. Fought to live.*

"Bailey!"

She woke up swinging, blindly smacking
her attacker. "Let me go!"

"Easy. Easy, B." She wasn't trapped in the
dark. There was no hood on her head. No
man in a surgical mask hovering above her.
She was in a bed. There was a lamp on beside
her. Granite-colored eyes blazed in the light.
"It's me, Spencer. Do you know me now?"

She took several more seconds to compre-
hend when and where she was. Not in the
past. Not in a windowless construction site
draped with plastic tarps. She was in Spencer Montgomery's home. On a winter's night.
She saw the scratches she'd raked across his
chest and felt his strong hands pinning her
wrists into her pillow.

"B?"

When she nodded, he released her and sat
up on the side of her bed.

"Sorry I had to hold you down," he apologized as she sat up and pushed her hair off
her face. "You were wailing pretty good on
me. I had to protect myself. I can tell you've

been working out." He winked. But she didn't see the humor. "I didn't hurt you, did I?"

He rubbed at his bare right shoulder. She'd done worse than scratch him? She climbed onto her knees beneath the sheet and blanket, and pushed the long sleeves of the black sweatshirt up past her elbows to free her hands before reaching out to brush her fingertips across the rusty-gold hair above his heart. "Did I hurt *you?*"

His muscle flinched as she neared the mark she'd made and he sucked in his breath, pulling away from her touch. "I can imagine who you were really fighting, and I hope you did hit him that hard." But he shook his head and pointed to the bruise on his tricep. "I jarred this pretty good diving into the parking garage this afternoon. But I heard you crying out, and..."

Now she saw the gun sitting on the table beside the lamp. He thought there'd been an intruder, that one of The Cleaner's hired thugs had gotten to her. Was that why she saw concern still lining his face?

"I'm okay. I'm safe. The nightmare woke me and I was disoriented, and it all got mixed together. I'm sorry I woke you." She looked up at the ceiling, knowing there were condos above and below them. "Do you think I woke anyone else?"

"We're pretty soundproofed here. Don't worry."

Bailey was breathing normally now and was fully able to distinguish memory from reality now. Her gaze was drawn back to his long, lean torso and she realized he'd charged to her rescue with nothing more than his gun and a pair of flannel pajama pants that rode temptingly low beneath his belly button.

And though her blood heated with a different kind of tension, it wasn't only longing that made her reach out to touch the puckered white scar that formed a jagged circle on his right flank. She'd seen something like that on a TV show—the scar from a bullet.

"What happened?" His flat stomach quivered when she touched his skin and Spencer shot to his feet.

"It's an old war wound." He picked up his gun and headed toward the door. "If you're okay, I'll go back and get some sleep now."

"Spencer." *Don't brush away my concern. Don't think I can't handle it.* Bailey swung her legs off the side of the bed, not bothering to pull the sweat pants back on over her panties as she hurried into the hallway after him. The shirt hit low enough on her thighs to make a modest nightgown. "I may not carry a badge or have a therapist's license, but I know how to listen."

She followed him straight into his bedroom, a carbon copy of the gray walls and dark wood downstairs.

"Don't come in here unless you intend to stay the night."

Bailey took another step in, stopping at the foot of his king-size bed while he circled around it. "Is that supposed to scare me away?"

"You make me feel things I haven't felt in a long time, Bailey. I don't know that I want to feel them."

"Because it hurts?" She was trying to piece together what he was admitting to her. "Something about the nightmare, about me crying out, bothered you."

"Let's see." He holstered his gun and set it on the bedside table before picking up the dove-gray comforter and shaking out the messy folds from his hasty dash to her room. "Someone tried to kill you today. She threatened to finish the job if you won't crawl into a hole and forget about the trial."

"Don't." Bailey snatched the cover from his hand and folded it back, out of his reach. "This isn't that relentless cop thing you do.

That scar means something. Tell me about it. Tell me what makes you so afraid to feel something for me."

When he turned around, there was a look of such pain and anguish on his chiseled face that Bailey immediately reached out.

He caught her hand, laced his fingers together with hers and pulled her half a step closer so that he could touch her, instead. One fingertip touched the bandage that closed the cut on her cheekbone, and then all five fingers sifted through her sleep-tossed hair to cup the side of her head.

"Can I keep you close tonight?" he asked. "Will it frighten you to have a man in your bed?"

Bailey leaned her cheek into the caress. "Not if it's you. And…" Her heart might be quick to answer, but she knew her limitations. "Not if we keep a light on."

Spencer turned off the overhead light, but left the lamp beside his bed on to cast a glow across the room as Bailey crawled in between the cool sheets. "Brr."

"Cold?" He gathered her into his arms without asking permission, and Bailey didn't mind a bit when she tumbled against a mile of skin and he rolled onto his side to face her. "Better?"

"Much." She rested her head on the pillow of his shoulder and quickly stopped shivering as the thick comforter and his tall, strong body cocooned her in a haven of warmth. But he was mistaken if he thought she was going to drift off to sleep. "Were you shot in the line of duty?"

He chuckled against her hair. "You go straight to the heart of things, don't you."

Bailey hadn't been intimate with a man since long before the rape, and she seemed to have forgotten where to rest her hands. But Spencer gently stopped them from dancing across his shoulders and waist, and held them against his chest where she could feel the strong beat of his heart beneath the ticklish dusting of hair.

"Back when I first made detective," he started, "I was assigned to an investigation. Money laundering through a restaurant. They were a front for organized crime."

"Sounds dangerous."

His heart beat a little faster. "The investigation was the easy part. It was pretty clear the owner was doctoring his books whenever he made a big wholesale foods purchase or catered a large event."

Bailey started tracing delicate circles across his skin, feeling antsy at how his story would end. "Did you have to deal with any of the mobsters?"

His chest expanded with a deep sigh, pushing Bailey slightly away. But he slid his hand beneath the sweatshirt and flattened his palm at the small of her back to keep her close. "That part comes later. I suppose the short version is that we convinced the owner's sister to testify against the men who were using her brother. Ellen was an accountant. She put two and two together when she paid the monthly bills. She knew the kind of men who came to the restaurant. She was afraid her brother would get hurt."

A woman. This was about a woman. Bailey's heart squeezed in her chest. Was this accountant the reason Spencer worked so hard to detach himself from his emotions?

"Who was Ellen to you?"

"I loved her." A painful gasp stuck in Bailey's throat. Spencer's hand moved beneath her shirt, trailing slowly up and down her back in a long, frictive caress. "Past tense, B. I loved her."

Once she'd moved past that jealous moment, or maybe once Spencer had calmed the thumping beat of his heart, he continued. "The D.A.'s office talked her into testifying against the men her brother worked for."

"Testify?" This time Bailey pushed away. But Spencer threw his top leg over both of hers to keep her close. And suddenly she understood that he needed her here. He needed the reassurance of her warmth. He needed the patience in her heart to open up this painful chapter of his past.

She stretched her left arm around his waist and nestled in beneath his chin.

"See any similarities?" His lips brushed against the crown of her hair.

"What happened to Ellen?" Bailey could already guess. But he needed to say it.

"We put her in a safe house right before the trial. I was one of the men assigned to protect her."

"Oh, Spencer. And I—"

"Shh."

He slipped a finger beneath her chin and tilted her face up to his. He pressed a soothing kiss to her lips. And though the stubble of his beard made it slightly rougher than he intended, the friction of it reminded Bailey of the contrasts between them—a man, a woman, lying close in bed in the heart of the night, sharing a hushed, private conversation. He kissed her again, stirring a response deep inside her.

"I lost my focus, B." The minimalist nickname was his alone for her. She felt uniquely linked to Spencer every time he said it.

There *was* a link between them. She couldn't care this deeply or trust this openly with a man she didn't share a special connection with. "Did Ellen die?"

His arms convulsed almost painfully tight around her and Bailey wanted to weep at the depth of what Spencer Montgomery could really feel. "She was afraid her brother would get if she testified. She'd changed her mind, but I don't think she knew how to tell me."

Changed her mind? "No wonder you didn't believe I'd stand up to Brian Elliott."

"Don't mention his name here. Not in this room. Ever."

Bailey pressed her lips against the pulse in Spencer's neck, and tasted salty, delicious heat.

"Ellen used my phone to call her brother. She thought he'd help her escape. But he came to the safe house with a bunch of thugs. They shot Ellen, her brother, a guard."

"You." She moved her lips to the taut underside of his chin, offering comfort, offering whatever he needed from her.

"She died in my arms because I didn't know how to love her *and* be a cop."

She kissed the marks she'd accidentally

scratched on his chest, wishing she could heal his fractured image of himself as easily as these would heal. "Spencer, you can't put that kind of burden on yourself."

He crushed her tight against his chest. "I should have saved her. What if something happens and I can't save you?"

Bailey squiggled some space between them and tipped her chin to look into those guilt-stricken eyes. "Life isn't easy, Spencer." She knew this secret far better than she ever would have liked. "Sometimes, stuff happens that isn't your fault, that you can't control. It doesn't mean you've failed or that you won't fail again. It just means that you have to fight harder. You have to be stronger. You can't let the bad stuff win. You have to keep getting up and moving forward even when you're afraid to or you don't think you can."

"B, don't say—"

"Something may happen to me."

"No."

"But it won't be your fault."

"I don't want to lose you!"

The words were so raw, so filled with an emotion that even Spencer himself didn't understand, that Bailey knew of only one thing to say.

"Then love me."

THAT WAS ONE order Spencer was willing to obey.

When Bailey lifted her lips to give him a kiss, he crushed his mouth over hers, accepting what she so generously offered, giving back all he could. He rolled her partly beneath him, running one hand beneath that sack of a sweatshirt she wore to touch the soft skin of her back, tangling the other hand in her even softer hair. He plunged his tongue into the silky warmth of her mouth and tasted her tongue sliding against his. He could get drunk on this woman's kisses—her dewy lips, their supple strength, their bold curiosity and unselfish welcome.

Her arms wound around his neck. Her fingers tunneled through his hair. She whimpered a seductive little hum in her throat that drew his lips to the tiny vibration of sound beneath her cool skin. His right hand roamed at will, dipping beneath the elastic of her panties to squeeze that roundly delicious bottom, sliding up the plane of her stomach to cup a taut, plump mound of flesh.

Bailey was at once a burning fire and a soothing balm. A classy lady and an irresistible siren. A gentle spirit and a passionate heart.

He knew Nick was in the lobby downstairs,

keeping watch over the building, allowing Spencer the respite he needed to sleep. But even more than rest, he needed to make love to the brave woman who'd set her own fears aside to listen to his. To share his pain. To understand his guilt. To heal his broken soul.

When he caught the turgid pearl at the tip of her breast and rolled it between his thumb and forefinger, she gasped aloud and buried her face against his chest. "Spencer..."

He instantly moved his hand to the more neutral territory of her back and pulled the heavy erection between his thighs away from the curve of her hip. "Did I hurt you?" he rasped, tilting her face up to read the truth in her eyes.

"No. It was...overwhelming. I'd forgotten."

Forgotten how good this could feel? Or forgotten how another man's hands had made her feel? "Did I frighten you? I don't want to do anything to remind you of him."

She silenced his apology with a finger over his lips. Then quickly replaced it with a soft, healing kiss. "He doesn't come into this room, remember?"

"That wasn't fair of me to say. I know you live with those memories every day. Have you even been with a man since then?"

She shook her head.

Spencer was hard with desire, but he'd take a cold shower before he'd do anything to hurt her. "Can you do this? Are you ready to be with a man?"

"I'm ready to be loved, not forced."

"Ah, hell, sweetheart." His lips went to hers again, reassuring her with everything in him that there was no other way he'd have her. "Tell me what you like. Tell me what you don't. Tell me to stop. Anytime. I'm not the most sensitive guy, but I can—"

"Could I be on top?" She whispered the request, the sweetest yes a man could know. "Is that okay?"

Rising up on one elbow, Spencer shucked the sweatshirt off over her head, removed her panties. She threw the covers back when he rolled away to pull a condom from the nightstand and sheathe himself. Then he lay back on the pillows, and pulled her over to straddle him, making himself as vulnerable to her as he knew how.

When she shyly covered her breasts from uncertainty or the chilled air, Spencer gently pried her hands away and brought them down to rest on the dancing, eager skin of his chest. She was porcelain and perfect from head to toe except for the rosy pink tips of her breasts, and the golden thatch of hair at her thighs.

Her beauty and trust were humbling things. "You mean you want me to be able to watch all this beautiful skin and touch these beautiful breasts and…"

Her breathing quickened as he did what he described. She rubbed her bottom against his shaft and he groaned with need.

"Do you want me?" she asked.

There were no other words. "Yes."

"That's what I need, Spencer. I need someone who wants me just because it's me."

"I need you." He pulled down to his chest for a kiss. With her breasts branding his chest, he lifted her bottom and slowly entered her tight, moist heat. "Ah, B," he growled, growing hard again as her body gripped him. "Ah, sweetheart."

She pushed herself up and he thrust inside her. "Spencer? That's good. I like that. I—"

When she closed her eyes and the tremors clutched him inside her, he was done talking. He thrust deeper, faster. He reached for her breasts and she covered his hands, linking their fingers together, squeezing them tight.

Bailey gasped his name as thrust himself up one last time and shook with the power of his own release.

Afterward, she collapsed on top of him and Spencer gathered her in his arms and pulled the comforter up to cover them both. They slept like that, with her spent body draped over his and his arms wrapped around her. And, for a few hours, Spencer Montgomery wasn't a cop.

For a few hours, at least, he was only a man in love.

Chapter Eleven

"I knew you'd look smashing in a tuxedo."

The compliment was genuine, but seemed to fall on deaf ears.

Bailey took Spencer's hand and stepped out of the SUV onto the cleared bricks leading up to the front steps of the Mayweather estate. Twin Christmas trees, festooned with white lights and crystal ornaments, framed the front door, with layers of snow filling the branches in such a way that it looked as if it had been placed there for a holiday magazine ad. A red carpet led the way past a grandstand of reporters into the wide marble foyer where she could see glimpses of white roses and evergreen garlands hanging with more lights inside. The music of a small chamber orchestra, playing both classical pieces and holiday tunes, danced softly on the chilling breeze.

It was everything a Christmas ball should

be. With lines of cars circling the driveway, dignitaries and wealthy guests pausing for pictures and sound bites before joining the party, it was everything her mother could want. It was probably everything Spencer loathed and it was an opportunity for Bailey.

Spencer handed his keys off to a parking valet she recognized as his partner, Nick Fensom. With a wink to Bailey and an "Everyone's in place" to Spence, he hurried around the hood to climb behind the wheel and drive away.

Bailey inhaled a deep breath through her nose and released the steaming air out through her carefully made-up lips. She hadn't expected tonight to be anything like a real date, but it might be reassuring to see at least a glimpse of the lover who'd bared his soul to her, and held her, skin to skin, in the warmth of his arms throughout the night.

It was important for her to be here—to calm her mother's fears that explosions and gunfire weren't any more of a threat than a Christmas card with an unpleasant message inside. She'd gotten the idea early this morning, as she'd lain in bed, snugged to Spencer's side, thinking. If she could manage her nightmares, overcome her fears of intimacy, and be the woman that a strong, confident man like Spencer Montgomery needed, then she could face the reporters, face her family, face the possibility of The Cleaner or one of her hired thugs showing up tonight to try to silence her one last time.

Without any usable leads panning out, it might be the only way the police could ferret out the Rose Red Rapist's accomplice and ensure the safety and success of his trial.

Spencer hated the idea. But he didn't have a better one.

Spencer tapped the bud in his ear and dipped his chin toward the lapel microphone that could have passed for a fraternity pin. "Montgomery here. I've got Bailey with me. We need eyes on her every minute tonight. If anyone senses anything out of place, I'm the first to know." She knew an unsettling thrill to be hanging on the arm of a man who conveyed such authority and generated such respect. She figured with Spencer was the safest place to be. Even if he doubted his ability to protect her now that things had gotten personal between them, she had no doubts. "Remember. Bailey and the guests are our first priority. If we can get this perp, do it. But we neutralize any threats to the civilians first. Understood?" A litany of responses buzzed in his ear. "Apprise Zeiss's men of our status. Montgomery out."

Bailey waited beside him, shivering beneath her midnight-blue wrap, fighting the cold air as much as her own trepidation about tonight. And about them.

Maybe Spencer could only allow a *them* for one night. Maybe he considered being with her a weakness he didn't want to repeat. Maybe he truly couldn't be both a cop and a man who cared.

The relentless cop had shown up to escort her to the ball tonight. The man she loved was buried somewhere deep under the starched white collar and gun and badge hidden beneath the trim fit of his suit.

If he wouldn't tell her that things would be okay, that the massive security and crowd of cameras and guests would keep her safe enough tonight, then maybe she should reassure him.

While he looked from side to side, taking note of the cars that had pulled up behind him and eyeing anyone who strayed too close, Bailey reached up to straighten his collar where the curling wire that connected his radio to the members of his task force had caught. "You said I could do anything I set my mind to."

He pulled her hand through the crook of his elbow and led her onto the red carpet. "Setting yourself up as bait and getting yourself killed for the trouble weren't what I had in mind."

"Spencer—"

"I know. You need to do this." His grip tightened and he pulled her aside, dropping his lips to her ear to whisper, "If anything happens tonight—if I'm not there for you—you fight. That's what you do, Bailey Austin. You get up and you fight."

Bailey reached up and brushed her fingertips along the cool line of his jaw. Maybe the man she loved *had* shown up tonight. "I will, Spencer," she promised. "Nose, throat, gut or groin. Keep moving. Keep fighting. I won't be the victim again."

He leaned in to press a kiss to her temple and Bailey tilted her head, savoring the tender touch.

Then the moment was over and he tugged her closer to his side as the cameras flashed. The cop was back. "Brace yourself. The fun's about to begin."

"Miss Austin?"

"Look this way!"

"Who are you with tonight?"

"How are you feeling?"

"Who are you wearing?"

"Any lasting effects from yesterday's attack?"

The rapid-fire barrage of snapshots and questions caught her off guard for a moment. But then she found her smile and the gracious genes she'd inherited from her mother, and paused for pictures and answered questions. She introduced Spencer, raved about her mother's decorations and reminded readers and viewers to donate as generously as they could afford.

When they reached the edge of the grandstand at the bottom of the stairs, a large television camera swung her way, capturing her in its spotlight. Vanessa Owen stepped forward with her microphone and Bailey dug her fingers into the fine wool of Spencer's sleeve, as wary of this encounter as she'd been the night the reporter had ambushed her in the KCPD parking garage.

"Happy Holidays, Miss Austin." The striking brunette wore a toasty-looking black coat with a fur-trimmed collar, and smiled into the camera as if she had no care about the frosty temps or her provocative questions. "How does it feel to know that an innocent woman was killed because of you? Maybe even killed because she was mistaken for you?"

"You're out of line, Miss Owen." Spencer tried to push past the reporter and camera, but Bailey was dragging her feet.

The shock and sadness of her neighbor's death washed over her anew. "Corie Rudolf was a friend of mine. I deeply mourn her passing and send my prayers to her family over their tragic loss."

But another emotion was growing inside her, too. The same emotion that had motivated her to say yes to the D.A.'s request to have the Rose Red Rapist's most prominent victim agree to testify, the same emotion that drove her to come here in the first place, the same emotion that made her want to shove Vanessa Owen's microwave right down the opportunistic brunette's throat.

Bailey smiled serenely, holding up her hand and interrupting before Vanessa could ask some other sensationalist question that was meant to get beneath her skin. "I am not to blame for Corie's murder. There's a woman called The Cleaner who has covered up crimes and destroyed people's lives and killed them…to help out a rapist. The same rapist who assaulted me."

"B—"

"*They* are the ones to blame. Not the victims." The anger, the helplessness and frustration, the stark, cold fear she hated to feel all rose to the surface and oozed out in succinct, daring words. "I blame The Cleaner for Corie's murder. And I think she ought to know that killing my friend only makes me more determined than ever to see that justice is done."

"Brave words for a person who's received how many threats? And you're still going to testify?"

"Yes."

Vanessa's predatory eyes narrowed. "Aren't you afraid The Cleaner will come after you again? Aren't you terrified?" The dark-haired woman leaned in. "Shouldn't we all be terrified that you're here with us tonight? Haven't you put all of us in danger?"

"We're all safe here," Spencer announced, even though he hadn't said those words to Bailey. "This interview is done."

Vanessa's phone rang as Spencer pushed Bailey past the last of the cameras. When she glanced back, she saw the look of irritation on the reporter's face as she read the incoming number.

"Yes?" she answered. "What? I can't. I'm on a live feed right now. Are you sure? Tonight?" She lifted her gaze to meet Bailey's at the top of the stairs. And held it. "That *would* be a fabulous story to tell." She repeated herself when the caller must have argued. "I'll take care of it." Then she disconnected the call and made a cutting gesture across her throat to tell her cameraman to turn off the feed.

"Spencer?" Bailey tugged on his sleeve when the reporter slipped through the cadre of reporters and disappeared from sight. "Where is she going?"

He pulled her inside to the marble foyer before answering. "Way to bait the trap, B. Challenging The Cleaner to come find you here?"

"Are you making a joke?"

"I'm on the job. I don't joke." His gray eyes were more probing than Vanessa's had been. "If she's not already here, she or her henchmen will be soon." He tapped the radio in his ear again. "Nick. Tell Zeiss's men to go on full alert. I think we're going to have a real party tonight. And somebody find me Vanessa Owen."

Bailey slipped off her wrap and moved on to the check-in table while Spencer relayed orders to his team. There were so many people here. The estate was huge, and nearly every room on the first floor was being used. Waitstaff moved through the guests, carrying trays of champagne and hors d'oeuvres. The musicians sat at one end of the open ballroom and dancers waltzed in a circle. There was a giant Christmas tree at the foot of the winding staircase where a professional photographer was snapping souvenir photos of the donors attending.

If The Cleaner was here, finding her wouldn't be easy. Bailey idly wondered if it would be just as difficult for The Cleaner to find her. She glanced back out at the reporters' stand. What if she already had? Vanessa Owen had once dated Brian Elliott. Would she still be loyal to him? Was she so hungry for a career-making story that she'd set up the very crimes she wanted to cover?

"Miss Austin?" A friendly voice diverted her attention away from the missing newswoman. Max Duncan, the bodyguard who'd nearly gotten arrested and had helped save her life, sat behind the table, wearing a suit and tie, an earbud like Spencer's, and those same reflective sunglasses he'd worn out in the snowy sunshine wrapped around the back of his neck. "How are you this evening?"

"Good, Max." She stretched up on tiptoe to look over the edge of the table and saw he was sitting on a stool with his leg out straight in a brace. A metal cane leaned against the table beside him. "How are you feeling?"

"Beat up and embarrassed. Dislocated my kneecap and cracked my shin bone." He read through the list of guests on his clipboard and checked off her name. "But it's all hands on deck with a party this big. I figured I could at least watch the door for Mr. Zeiss tonight. I need to get back on his nice list."

Bailey smiled. "It's good to see you in one piece."

"Yes, ma'am. You, too." Max's gaze strayed up to greet the red-haired man brushing his hand against Bailey's back. She startled at the faintly possessive touch, and was disappointed when Spencer pulled away just as quickly. "Detective." Max picked up his clipboard again and found Spencer's name. "You carrying?"

"Yes." Spencer nodded and pulled back his jacket to reveal the gun holstered there before buttoning it shut again. "You've got a registration of everyone else here who's carrying a weapon?"

Max made another check on his list. "Your people. And all the Zeiss personnel. We're the ones in the gray uniforms." He patted the brace on his thigh. "I, personally, won't get there very fast. But we'll come running if you need us."

Spencer thanked him. "Good to know."

"Bailey!"

Bailey groaned as her mother called to her from the photographer's station and swept across the foyer in a sashay of wine-red taffeta. "Now it's my turn to say, 'Brace yourself.'"

Linking her arm through Spencer's, Bailey crossed to the foot of the staircase to meet Loretta Austin-Mayweather halfway. Her mother hugged her, carefully turning her cheek so as not to smudge either of their makeup. "I'm so glad you came. This color is divine on you. Darling, let me look at you."

Loretta caught Bailey's hands and leaned back, zeroing in on the bandage on her cheek. "Oh, dear. I knew you'd been hurt." She touched her fingers to the bruising cut and frowned. "Will that leave a scar?" Before Bailey could answer, she pulled her over to the photographer, who snapped a candid photo of them both. By the time the after-image of the flash had cleared Bailey's retinas, Loretta was already pointing to her injury. "This can be edited out of the pictures, can't it?"

"Yes, ma'am."

Loretta had her by the hand again, pulling her toward the ballroom. "I want you to come say hello to the mayor."

"Mother?" Bailey planted her feet. She didn't care about scars in pictures or scoring points with local politicians. But she did care that her mother acknowledge the danger her daughter was facing, and maybe, just maybe, find the strength to show a little compassion. "You remember my friend Spencer."

"Your friend?" Loretta's tone was decidedly less welcoming than her eagerness to see Bailey had been. "Detective Montgomery."

"Mrs. Mayweather."

"Mother. I dressed up and came to your party for you. Be nice."

Something like despair put instant lines on Loretta's delicate features. She reached out to squeeze Spencer's hand. "Thank you for saving my daughter's life." Then the lines vanished and she pointed a stern finger at him. "But if your people do anything to ruin this fund-raiser, you're not going to be in tonight's family portrait."

SPENCER WOULD BE happy to dance every dance with Bailey for the rest of the evening. While it was pure torture to hold her in his arms and concentrate on something besides the way the color of her dress deepened the blue of her eyes or how the summery scent of her hair followed him with every twirl around the floor, at least she was in his arms. Locked down tight, her location secure.

But he'd spent as many dances standing on the sidelines, watching her chat up the deputy commissioner, a retired real estate developer and a player from the chief's football team. He'd catch his breath when he lost sight of her behind a taller dancer, breathe easier once those sunny-gold curls reappeared.

She'd make a fine wife for any man who wanted to move up the corporate ladder or make chief or commissioner one day. She'd be a finer wife for any man who wanted a true partner—a woman whose strengths and talents complemented his own, whose gentle heart and tenacious spirit could ease a man's troubled spirit or ignite the fires of passion inside him.

Spencer squeezed his eyes shut as the longing hit him again. He just had to get her through tonight. He had to get her through tomorrow. He had to get her to that trial on Monday, and then maybe he could decide if he could get through a life with Bailey at his side. But as long as she was in danger, as long as The Cleaner was out there, could he really risk…

Spencer opened his eyes and felt his heart skip a beat when he didn't see her. "B?"

He quickly scanned the dance floor. Couples spun by him in a Viennese waltz. But no dark blue gown. No golden hair.

He was crossing the room to the corner where he'd last seen her. His fingertip was at his ear to call for backup when he spotted her dancing out the door into the foyer with a black-haired man.

Oh, no, no, no, no, no. Spencer crossed straight out the ballroom's second door to cut off Gabriel Knight before he could corner Bailey and grill her with the same accusatory questions Vanessa Owen had, or throw out another of those *poor little rich girl* cracks. But as he excused his way through a group of laughing, chatting guests, Spencer saw that Gabe Knight wasn't questioning Bailey at all.

Knight was introducing Bailey to his date, his boss, Mara Boyd-Elliott. The platinum blonde was sitting behind one of the dozens of Christmas trees decorating the house. Her head was bent toward a sheaf of papers in her lap. She signed her name to one and pushed the documents off to the brunette sitting beside her, standing as Bailey approached. "Miss Austin."

Seriously? That was one screwed-up ex-family dynamic. What was Regina Hollister doing here? Judging by the business jacket and slacks she wore, she hadn't received an invitation.

But she did seem eager to reclaim Mara's attention. "Ms. Boyd, if you could finishing signing—"

"Regina, please," the blonde woman snapped. "This isn't my office. This is a social event. We're celebrating the holidays."

Regina exhaled a weary sigh that puffed the dark bangs off her forehead. "I understand that, ma'am, and I'm sorry to intrude. But I'm trying to help Brian take care of things before the…" Her gaze darted to Bailey and she rephrased her explanation with a bit of a sneer. "Before Monday." She held out the pen and documents one more time. "He needs your signature on these shared asset forms so we can get the property liquidated before the end of the year. Please."

"Oh, very well." With a flourish that was more style than business, Mara grabbed the papers and signed each copy before dropping them back in Regina's hands.

"Thank you, Ms. Boyd. I know he'll appreciate it." She included Bailey and Knight, as well, as she picked up her coat and briefcase and hurried toward the front door. "Enjoy your evening."

So what did Mara have to say to Bailey? Apologize for ever helping her scumbag of an ex get out of jail? Ask if she'd do an interview for her newspaper?

Or maybe this meeting was Bailey's idea. "Do you still do business with your ex-husband?"

"It was an amicable divorce, Miss Austin. We've continued a mutually beneficial working relationship ever since."

"I said to leave the detective work to me," Spencer grumbled. But as long as he had eyes on Bailey...and the suspect was talking.

Spencer hung back at the fringe of the other group and listened to the snippets of hushed, urgent conversation he could hear.

Good girl. Bailey hugged her arms around her middle, keeping her distance from both Knight and Mrs. Elliott. "Why are you telling me this?" she asked.

Mara Boyd was pleading her case with Bailey, it sounded like. "Because you don't know Brian the way I do."

"I'm certain we don't." Bailey shook her

head. "How could you ever help someone like that?"

"He's not well. That's one reason we still own properties jointly—" she gestured toward the front door "—one reason Regina is working weekends to take care of his paperwork. We're trying to protect his best interests." The older woman reached for Bailey's hand, but she cringed away. Rebuffed, Mara tucked her arm through Gabe Knight's and leaned against him, instead. "When I inherited the paper and my father's fortune, something changed with Brian. He was a self-made man. Suddenly, I eclipsed him. I wasn't the helpmate he wanted any longer. I think he saw me as competition. I know he resented my success."

"That's a sad story," Bailey said. "But it doesn't change what he did to me."

"No, but…" Mara sat back down and Spencer inched up to the tree to hear what she had to say. "I'm a smart woman, Miss Austin. I can do the math. The rapes started right after I divorced Brian. I'm the reason he hates women. Everything that he's done is my fault."

What she was sharing with Bailey was merely circumstantial, not any kind of conclusive evidence. Spencer had heard enough.

The woman was trying to assuage her own guilt. And she didn't need to be dumping that on Bailey. "Then that makes you another victim, Mrs. Elliott." He circled around Knight and slid his arm behind Bailey's waist. "Or an accomplice. Is there some information about your ex that you've been withholding from the police throughout this whole investigation? For example, did he ever display any of those violent rages when he was with you? Did he hurt you?"

"My ex-husband is a sick man," she reiterated. "I'm trying to protect him. I owe him that." She stood and linked her arm through Knight's. "Gabriel, I think I'd like to leave now."

Once they'd gone, Spencer released Bailey and turned to face her. "What part of don't go off by yourself don't you understand? Let me talk to Mara Elliott, Regina Hollister and Gabe Knight. You don't need to get that close to those people."

"I thought she could be The Cleaner. You heard her. She wants to protect her ex. She's probably paying his attorney's fees for him, too. I bet that's why she's liquidating those properties."

"You need to stop finding suspects for

me. I've already got a team trying to track down where Vanessa Owen disappeared to." Spencer exhaled a deep breath and rubbed his hands up and down her arms, trying to keep the fear of her getting hurt pushed down deep where it couldn't distract him. It was one job he was discovering he wasn't very good at. "Look, B—it's one thing to try to lure this woman out. It's something else when you purposely go looking for trouble."

Bailey's hands settled at his chest and played with his tie. He recognized the little caresses as an attempt to soothe his concern. "I wasn't looking for trouble. I just want answers. Besides, I wasn't alone. The guard was right over there." She turned to prove her point, but the table in the foyer was empty. "Max?"

"Behind you." He limped across the marble tiles, leaning heavily on his cane. "Detective Montgomery, we've got a situation."

"Not again," Bailey whispered beside him.

Spencer reached for her hand as the bodyguard pulled a green envelope from inside his jacket and handed it over. It had already been placed inside a clear plastic bag, preserving any trace for evidence. But the card was familiar and the message was all too clear.

I warned you.

Now you've ruined your mother's Christmas.

"When? How?" Bailey's fingers convulsed around his.

"We found it in the donation basket under the ballroom Christmas tree," Max reported. "We've been changing the basket out every hour so we can put the checks and cash in the safe. That means your suspect has been here in the past twenty minutes or so."

Spencer surveyed the number of guests and staff in the house. Maybe fifty in the foyer. Another two hundred in the ballroom. There were people in the dining room and game room. Staff in the kitchen and throughout the rest of the house. "She's probably still here. Any sign of a bomb?"

"Not yet. I talked to Mr. Zeiss and our people have begun a low-key evacuation. We're stationed at all the exits. We're telling guests in small groups that we've detected a gas leak and that a repair crew is on its way." Max unbuttoned his suit jacket at the same time Spencer did. Both men wanted quick access to their firearm if needed. "I'm on my way to inform Mr. Mayweather now."

"Have him make an announcement in the ballroom. We need to clear the estate in an orderly manner without anyone getting hurt." And without such a rush to the exits that their perp escaped, too.

"Nick, she's here." He alerted the task force members on his radio. "We're evacuating the house. But don't let any of the guests leave."

"Understood."

Spencer wound his arm around Bailey's shoulders and turned her toward the front door. "Let's get you out of here, too."

Before they could take another step, all the lights went out and the first woman screamed.

BAILEY FELT SPENCER pushing her against the wall beside one of the Christmas trees, shielding her with his body as several guests panicked and ran from the ballroom, bumping into and tripping over the people who were already there.

A violin screeched and the music suddenly stopped. She heard curses and cries of pain. A glass crashed and shattered on the hard floor. Someone was crying. There were more screams and people shouting for loved ones, the excited chatter of hundreds of people talking all at once. She heard footsteps running toward the back of the house, others shifting like restless cattle.

She heard Jackson's voice in the ballroom,

shouting to be heard above the chaos. "Everyone, remain calm. Stay where you are." He hollered for Zeiss and his crew to get them some light and the sounds of worried voices swelled. "Please, people."

"If anyone gets hurt…" Bailey clung to the walnut paneling, hating the frightened sounds she could hear. "Did I ever tell you I'm afraid of the dark? That Brian Elliott put a hood over my head when he wasn't…"

"Shh." Firm lips warmed the nape of her neck. "Just focus on the sound of my voice." Spencer moved behind her. He pulled out his cell phone and punched up an app that lit up the screen with a bright light. "Here." Suddenly, there was a small beam of light shining at her feet. "See? We're not in the dark."

Following the illumination of his phone light, Bailey could see other guests and the Zeiss security guards turning on phones and flashlights, transforming the dark night of the powerless house into a dim twilight.

Still, Bailey didn't breathe any easier until Spencer took her hand and pulled her into step beside him. He stretched his long arm over his head, forming a beacon that several people came closer to. "I'm Detective Montgomery, KCPD," he announced. "I need everyone to stay calm. I'm going outside to see if my people can tell me anything about the power outage. Please stay where you are."

He slowly made his way toward the front door, but he'd made the mistake of announcing his authority and the frightened guests were following in their wake like lemmings to a seaside cliff.

"Stay put, people," he reminded them, but they were gathering around, closing in. From all directions now.

A man jostled Bailey's arm. "Spencer?"

Someone bumped her again and she lost hold of Spencer's hand. "Spence?"

"Bailey?"

She reached for him again, but suddenly she was being pushed back. More people were drifting into the foyer from the ballroom now, separating her from her savior like a deep, rushing stream.

"Bailey?" He swung his light around, illuminating her face in the crowd. But they were moving farther and farther apart.

He flipped his light in a different direction, back to the ballroom's second archway. "Duncan! Can you reach her?"

A second beam of light hit Bailey from behind. "I got her."

"Bailey, I'll meet you outside."

"Okay."

The burly bodyguard pushed aside the people in his way and closed his hand around Bailey's arm. "Let's get you out of here."

Bailey nodded, eager to stay with a light and a friendly face. "What about my wrap? It'll be freezing outside."

Max tugged out of the path of an elderly couple feeling their way along the wall. "Cloakroom's the other direction. I'll take you out the back. I'll loan you my jacket if we can't find something along the way."

The crowd thinned as they cleared the ballroom exodus and Bailey realized Max was walking at a quicker pace than he had earlier this evening. And he wasn't using his cane. "You must be feeling better."

He held up the cane and shrugged. "I kept tripping people."

She smiled, appreciating his attempt to alleviate her concern. What she didn't appreciate was his grip tightening around her arm. Any more force and he'd be leaving bruises. She patted his hand. "Hey, lighten up. I can keep up now."

The first tinge of disquiet hit when he didn't loosen his grip.

The second came when he picked up the pace, walking just as quickly as she could on two uninjured legs. "Max?"

This was wrong. Something was very wrong.

Be aware of your surroundings, Bailey.

She knew she was in trouble when he turned off into a smaller hallway before they reached the kitchen. She tugged against his grip, but he wasn't stopping. "I grew up in this house, Max. This isn't the way—"

He pushed open a secluded door and shoved her inside.

She tumbled off one of her heels, wrenching her ankle, but it wasn't enough pain to stop her from charging toward the door and pummeling the muscle-bound bully who'd put her here. "Damn it, Max, it's as dark as a closet in here. Where's your flashlight?"

"Here's your light." Another voice. A woman's voice.

Bailey spun around.

"What?" Suddenly, there was a bright light shining in her eyes, blinding her after the darkness. Bailey shielded her eyes against the sharp beam of the LED flashlight and squinted at the face that went with the woman's voice into focus. "You're...Regina Hollister." Brian

Elliott's executive assistant. Always lurking in the background whenever her employer was around. The papers she'd brought for Mara Boyd-Elliott to sign had probably been fakes. She hadn't come to the ball for a signature. She'd come for her. "What are you doing here?"

"Cleaning up a mess. Just like I clean up all of Brian's messes. He needs me for that, you know. From the time we started building his company together, I've always taken care of whatever he needs."

The Cleaner.

Instinctively, Bailey backed away from the woman's cold, unsmiling stare. But in the small butler's pantry, she quickly bumped into Max. He hadn't budged when she'd struck a moment earlier, so she tried pleading. "Please call Spencer. Whatever this woman is holding over you, whatever she's paying—it's not worth it. I'll double whatever she's paying you."

"Max," Regina warned. "We have a schedule to keep."

Even in the dim tunnel of illumination inside the room, she could see the regret stamped on Max's bulldog features. "It isn't the money, Miss Austin. I'm sorry I have to do this."

"Do what?" The rustling of her long dress was the only sound for several long seconds.

Then a soft cloth came down over her head and she was plunged into utter darkness. Bailey screamed. The flashback to fear was instant and overwhelming. But she was a different woman now than she'd been that night.

She bit down on the hand that covered her mouth. Max swore. She pushed off the hood, but his hands were on her again. Bailey punched up, catching him in the throat. When he grabbed her by the hair, she clawed at his hands, clawed at his face. Her fingers fisted around those ridiculous sunglasses he'd worn tonight and she ripped them from his neck, tossing them away into the shadows.

"Damn it, Miss Austin, quit fightin' me."

"You're wasting my time. Give me that." Something long and hard struck Bailey in the back of the head, driving her to her knees and knocking her woozy.

"Spencer," she murmured, feeling the floor rush up to meet her. "I need you."

She was vaguely aware of her wrists and legs being bound, of the hood sliding over her face. Her head felt like a swinging cannonball when Max picked her up over his shoulder.

This was her nightmare all over again— struck from behind, bound—her world reduced to the blackness inside the hood. Only one thing remained in the re-creation of that horrible night.

The last thing she heard was Regina's clipped, matter-of-fact voice. "Bring her. He wants to see her before I finish her off."

Chapter Twelve

Spencer stood in the doorway of the butler's pantry holding a twisted pair of sunglasses and the midnight-blue heel of Bailey's shoe.

He'd known she was gone long before they'd gotten the power back on and had cleared the entire mansion. If she was here, she'd have been right by his side, right in the middle of things—asking questions, straightening his tie, adding light to his dark old soul, listening, loving, standing up to make a difference.

But it had taken twenty minutes longer for the Zeiss security guard to report the drops of blood on the rug back there. It wasn't enough blood to indicate a serious injury, but it was enough to know that she hadn't gone willingly.

Keep fighting, sweetheart.

Now he just had to get to her in time.

Losing Bailey the way he'd lost Ellen wasn't something a man could survive.

Spencer unhooked his tie and loosened his collar. Time to go to work.

"What do we know?"

Hans, the muscular German Shepherd who partnered with big Pike Taylor, was panting in the hallway. Pike rubbed the dog's muzzle and ears, rewarding him for completing his task. "Hans followed the trail to the staff parking lot where Max Duncan's truck was parked. He had enough of a scent to get us out to the highway. They turned east, into the city."

"The only prints are Max Duncan's on the door knob." Annie Hermann pulled a giant pair of tweezers from her crime-scene kit and plucked a tiny filament from the rug. "I've got a black thread."

"They put a hood on her." Spencer couldn't prove it, but he knew how to put together the pieces of the puzzle. The hood was part of the Rose Red Rapist's M.O. His stomach twisted into knot. The darkness? The disorientation? Bailey would be terrified.

Nick's gut had him sniffing the air at the back of the pantry. "Do you smell that? Perfume. Unless it's Bailey's?"

"No." Bailey was clean, fresh, citrusy sunshine. "It's hers. The Cleaner's."

Nick's phone buzzed on his belt and he

read the information there. "Got a text from Sarge. Once we narrowed the search to Duncan, she got a hit. Apparently, Duncan has a past he'd like to keep in the past. That's how she got him to turn on Bailey." He flipped open the key pad and replied, "I'll tell Sarge to put an APB out on his truck."

Kate Kilpatrick waited in the hallway. "I talked to Bailey's parents and got a list of all the women invited to the party and any female press or staff who were on their checklist."

Pike stood up beside her. "But if Duncan's the guy checking her in at the door, he wouldn't put her on that list."

"Here's the kicker." Kate opened a manila file and pulled out a photograph. "Loretta Mayweather is a wreck with her daughter missing—but that woman knows her guest list. I had her look through the pictures the photographer took, to help us match names to faces, and she spotted this." She handed the photo to Spencer. "The one person here tonight she didn't invite."

"The one person not dressed for a formal occasion." Spencer brushed his fingertip over the image of Bailey in the middle of her conversation with Mara Boyd-Elliott and Gabriel

Knight. But he was looking at the fourth person in that photograph.

The one wearing slacks and a jacket.

Regina Hollister.

The Cleaner.

Spencer handed the picture off to Nick and the others. "Let's go get her."

FIGHT. THAT'S what you do. You fight.

Spencer's voice filled Bailey's thoughts when she came to on top of the plastic-covered mattress for the second time.

She rolled onto her side, facing the voices she could hear, hating the sound of the crinkling plastic almost as much as she hated the hood that had kept her in darkness earlier.

She wasn't quite sure how she could take care of herself with her wrists bound and her head throbbing from the knot on the back of her scalp. A long silk gown with one shoulder and too many stays wasn't exactly her regular workout gear, either.

But she wasn't giving up. Spencer would be looking for her. He was smart and observant and knew how to get the best from the people he led. He'd figure it out. He'd find her.

She wasn't going to be another tragedy weighing heavily on his noble heart.

Bailey tilted her gaze to the discarded leg brace and cane lying on the floor beside the stack of lumber where Max Duncan sat, guarding her. Meanwhile, Brian Elliott and Regina Hollister stood with their heads bowed together over the workbench in the far corner of the construction site—laughing and plotting and not looking anything much like a boss and his assistant.

The sun must be up by now, although there wasn't a single window in this demolished section of some floor in some old building that was being renovated by Elliott's company. He owned dozens of buildings across the city.

But Spencer would find her. He would be there for her.

The setting was disturbingly familiar. An old warehouse, stripped down to the studs, covered in layers of plastic. She sat on a plastic-covered mattress in the middle of the floor.

The only difference was that Elliott was allowing her to see her surroundings in detail this time. He was allowing her to see his face without any effort to disguise it.

She knew the only reason they'd let her take off the hood and see the details of her surroundings was that they had no intention of letting her leave here alive.

"Why are you doing this, Max?" she asked, needing to do something before the fear or helplessness got too strong a hold on her again.

"I've done some things in my past I'm not too proud of. They could cost me my job." He laughed, but it wasn't a pleasant sound. "Let's just say I haven't always made a living with my clothes on."

"Oh." She hadn't expected that answer from the tough guy she'd once vouched for with the police. But then she supposed she didn't much care about the choices he'd had to make, since they'd led to her being held prisoner. Surely, Brian Elliott didn't think he could get away with the star witness in the case against him.

But then, maybe that's exactly what he thought. As difficult as The Cleaner had been for Spencer's task force to identify and capture, maybe Regina had a plan that would allow Brian to get away without any blame. After all, who was going to argue his guilt but one dead victim and a weak man being blackmailed into silence?

"What about Corie?" Bailey ignored the ringing in her skull and the throbbing in her injured cheek when she pushed herself up to a sitting position. "She had a crush on you, you know. It wouldn't have mattered to her who you are or where you've been."

Max leaned forward, bracing his elbows on his knees and resting his chin on his hands.

Brace. He'd removed his leg brace entirely and tossed it to the floor near the edge of her mattress. Maybe he'd never been injured at all, and it had simply been a ruse to gain her trust and give him access to her mother's guest list last night.

"I'm sorry about your friend. She was a sweet kid." Bailey scooted to the edge of the mattress and dropped her feet over the side, gathering her long skirt around her legs. "She was spying on you, too. Between her and me we had eyes on you almost around the clock."

"I had no idea." Now that hurt. Two people she'd trusted. Two people who'd betrayed her.

Come on, Spencer.

Bailey dropped the hem of her dress down around her feet, letting the edge fall over part of the cane. "So was she killed because she looked like me and someone made a mistake? Or was she collateral damage?"

"Neither. Corie was getting cold feet." Max's attention drifted over to the far side of the room to the two conscienceless tyrants who didn't give a whit about anyone else's lives but their own. "I don't think she wanted to see you get hurt."

Bailey curled her toes around the cane and pulled it out of sight beneath her dress. "I don't suppose Regina lets you change your mind about helping her."

"If Regina wants something, she calls you. And if you don't do what she asks, she finds you." Max snorted a derisive laugh through his nose. "We're just pawns. It's all about Mr. Elliott for her. That is one sick relationship. She's lover, mother, caretaker, protector to him."

"What does he do for her?" Weapon? Check. The cane seemed to have done a decent job on the back of her own head. Bailey stretched out her arms, making a show of flexing her fingers while she got her feet planted flat on the plastic tarp beneath them.

"I'm not sure. The money. The job."

Bailey reached down for the cane and came up swinging. Nose. *Pop!* She heard the cartilage give when she smacked it across Max's face. Holding his bleeding face, cursing, he pushed to his feet. Throat. She swung again, catching him in the Adam's apple and knocking him back to his seat.

"Max!" Regina shouted a warning.

"Stop her!" That was Elliott.

Gut. Max fell backward over the stack of wood and Bailey brought the cane down hard in his midsection, stealing the wind from his belly.

The split second she paused to decide whether to hold on to the cane or go for the gun in his belt was the split second it took for Brian Elliott to reach her.

She screamed when his arms clamped around her body, lifting her off her feet. He shook her like a rag doll until the cane dropped from her hands. After kicking it away, he threw Bailey back onto the mattress and was on top of her before she could scramble away.

"Get off me!" She scratched at his face, gouged at his eyes. "Get off!"

"Oh, yeah. This is what I wanted." He pulled at the folds of her skirt, shoving the silk and petticoats up to her thighs. Bailey twisted, screamed.

"Shut her up!" Regina yelled behind him. "Someone will hear."

Ignoring the warning, Elliott gave her a command. "Bring my kit."

Bailey heard Max moaning, footsteps running.

"You should have let me take care of her,"

Regina insisted. "I could have made this problem all go away."

"Don't tell me what to do!"

"Here." Regina dropped a toolbox beside the mattress. "I hear sirens."

"Spencer!" Bailey yelled in desperation. "Help!"

A hard slap across the face silenced her plea. Bailey felt her mind sliding back to that night. To this place.

She'd tried to fight. But her head hurt. Her arms were so tired.

Elliott rubbed his hands together and she realized he'd squirted some kind of disinfectant onto them. "Of all the women who have dared to defy me, you have been the most brazen." He covered the chemical smell with the wretched cologne that sent her straight back to that night.

"Stop. Please," she begged.

"Brian." Bailey saw Regina come up behind Brian and touch his shoulder. "The police are downstairs. You have to get out now."

Police? "Spencer!"

Fight. That's what you do. You fight.

"Not until I'm finished!" He shrugged off the warning and ripped at the seam of Bailey's gown. "Calling me out in the press? Picking me out of a police lineup?"

"You raped me!"

"You needed it."

Bailey had one move left. Groin.

"Brian!"

Her attacker fell onto the floor, writhing in pain, and Bailey rolled off the mattress on the opposite side, pulling down her clothes, pushing to her feet.

"Max, get up! Get rid of her! Brian?" Regina knelt on the floor beside the man she idolized. "Darling?"

"KCPD! We're coming in!"

A loud pop and the cracking of wood filled Bailey's ears as she lurched toward the door.

"Spencer!"

"Bailey!"

She caught sight of his red-gold hair. An army followed him through the door and fanned across the room, each targeting a different kidnapper.

"KCPD! Get on the ground! Now!"

A dog's fierce barking drowned out the words.

Brian Elliott cursed. "Get that slavering dog away from me!"

"You found me." Bailey rushed forward, needing Spencer's arms around her now. "Thank God, you—"

Bailey jerked back, stumbling at the sudden shift in movement, as Regina snatched the back of her dress. The taller woman wound her forearm around Bailey's neck and pulled her in front of her body to use her as a human shield.

Regina must have recovered Max's gun, or had carried one all along, because there was definitely a hard metal gun barrel pressing into Bailey's temple.

"Everybody, stop!" Spencer ordered. "B?"

His gray eyes flickered over Bailey's face, then hardened when they met the threat in Regina's. But his arms had frozen in the air, his gun cradled between his hands.

"I missed on purpose last time," Regina taunted. "Thought I could scare some sense into your little girlfriend here." Bailey cringed as the woman pressed the gun against her cheek. "You let Brian go—" Regina slid the gun to Bailey's temple "—or I won't miss again."

Bailey's eyes stung with tears at the anguish that lined Spencer's face. She could see the nightmare in his eyes. But his first love had surrendered. She hadn't trusted him enough to keep her safe. "I'm not Ellen, Spence," she said simply, filling her eyes and her voice with all the love and trust she had for him. "You aren't going to lose me."

"Isn't that sweet? Don't worry, Brian." Regina ground the gun into Bailey's temple, hard enough to tilt her head to the side. Brian Elliott was already in handcuffs. But Regina would clean up his mistakes right up to the very end. "I promise Miss Austin will never testify against you."

It was a promise Regina would never keep.

Spencer fired his gun. Bailey jerked at the first shot. But Regina's grip on her went slack.

"Get down, B!" Spencer marched forward as Bailey ducked and Nick Fensom pulled her safely out of the line of fire.

Regina pulled the trigger, but her shot went wide. Spencer fired two more times and Regina Hollister crumpled in a heap, dead.

Finally, he lowered his gun. "B?"

"Spencer!" Bailey ran to him. "Spence—"

He claimed her mouth in a kiss that was hot and hard and over far too quickly. But his arm anchored her to his side. She lifted her fingers to straighten the collar that was hopelessly twisted with the hanging tail of his tie. He leaned down to rest his forehead against hers. "We got 'em, sweetheart. The bad guys didn't get to win."

They stood there like that for several seconds, his eyes searching her face. Finally, he raised his head, although the arm around her remained. He looked to the other members of his team. "We need to clear the prisoners out of here and secure the scene. Get Annie up here with her kit and call—"

"We got it, boss," Nick teased. "We can handle a crime scene." He pulled Max Duncan to his feet and winked at Bailey. "Be gentle with this one, Bails."

"Out!" Spencer ordered.

Pike Taylor led Brian Elliott out the door and Nick followed.

Spencer started to say something. But with Regina Hollister's dead body in the room—or maybe because he didn't quite know what to say, either, now that the threat to Bailey had been neutralized and there was no need for a relentless cop to protect her anymore—he touched the cut on her cheek and sighed.

Next, he holstered his weapon and shrugged out of his jacket. Like the true gentleman he was, Spencer draped it around her shoulders and took her by the hand.

He led her down a flight of stairs and they made a bracing dash to his SUV. After killing the emergency lights, he turned on the engine, cranked the heat and pulled her into his lap so he could capture her mouth in a deep, potent kiss. Bailey wound her arms around his neck, riding the deep rise and fall of his chest—answering him touch for touch, kiss for kiss, until they were generating plenty of heat on their own.

When they came up for air, Spencer framed her face between his hands and looked into her eyes. "I know you want to change the world and doing something meaningful and take care of yourself. Those are mighty big dreams for a man to compete with. But I need you, B. Please let that be enough."

Bailey stroked her fingers across his lips, quieting the raw urgency in his voice. "You *do* love me, don't you, detective?" she asked, feeling one little bit of uncertainty. "Don't let me be the only one feeling this way."

Spencer pulled her back to his chest, tunneling his fingers into her hair. "Yes, I love you. I want to marry you. I know with the rape, you need recovery time. And then everything you've been through this week, and the trial to deal with. I'm a patient man. I'll give you all the time you need, all the space you want until you're ready to say yes."

"Yes," Bailey answered without hesitation, snuggling into Spencer's arms, feeling safe, strong, perfect. "Yes."

WHEN DWIGHT POWERS called her name, Bailey released her grip on Spencer's hand. She walked past the defense's table, looking beyond Kenna Parker's stoic expression to meet Brian Elliott's hateful, condemning eyes.

But Spencer's steady, granite-colored gaze was there for her when she turned to face the courtroom. His engagement ring was on her finger. She stepped into the witness's stand beside the judge's bench and raised her right hand.

"Do you solemnly swear to tell the truth, the whole truth, and nothing but the truth, so help you God?"

Bailey answered, "I do."

* * * * *

Coming in 2014
ONCE A COP
The next thrilling romantic
suspense novel from
THE PRECINCT
by USA TODAY Bestselling Author
Julie Miller
Only from Harlequin Intrigue

Reader Service.com

Manage your account online!
- Review your order history
- Manage your payments
- Update your address

*We've designed
the Harlequin® Reader Service
website just for you.*

Enjoy all the features!
- Reader excerpts from any series
- Respond to mailings and
  special monthly offers
- Discover new series available to you
- Browse the Bonus Bucks catalog
- Share your feedback

Visit us at:

ReaderService.com

RS13

LARGER-PRINT BOOKS!

GET 2 FREE
LARGER-PRINT NOVELS
PLUS 2 FREE
MYSTERY GIFTS

Love Inspired®
SUSPENSE
RIVETING INSPIRATIONAL ROMANCE

Larger-print novels are now available...

YES! Please send me 2 FREE LARGER-PRINT Love Inspired® Suspense novels and my 2 FREE mystery gifts (gifts are worth about $10). After receiving them, if I don't wish to receive any more books, I can return the shipping statement marked "cancel." If I don't cancel, I will receive 4 brand-new novels every month and be billed just $5.24 per book in the U.S. or $5.74 per book in Canada. That's a savings of at least 23% off the cover price. It's quite a bargain! Shipping and handling is just 50¢ per book in the U.S. and 75¢ per book in Canada.* I understand that accepting the 2 free books and gifts places me under no obligation to buy anything. I can always return a shipment and cancel at any time. Even if I never buy another book, the two free books and gifts are mine to keep forever.

110/310 IDN F5CC

Name	(PLEASE PRINT)

Address	Apt. #

City	State/Prov.	Zip/Postal Code

Signature (if under 18, a parent or guardian must sign)

Mail to the **Harlequin® Reader Service:**
IN U.S.A.: P.O. Box 1867, Buffalo, NY 14240-1867
IN CANADA: P.O. Box 609, Fort Erie, Ontario L2A 5X3

**Are you a current subscriber to Love Inspired Suspense books
and want to receive the larger-print edition?
Call 1-800-873-8635 or visit www.ReaderService.com.**

* Terms and prices subject to change without notice. Prices do not include applicable taxes. Sales tax applicable in N.Y. Canadian residents will be charged applicable taxes. Offer not valid in Quebec. This offer is limited to one order per household. Not valid for current subscribers to Love Inspired Suspense larger-print books. All orders subject to credit approval. Credit or debit balances in a customer's account(s) may be offset by any other outstanding balance owed by or to the customer. Please allow 4 to 6 weeks for delivery. Offer available while quantities last.

Your Privacy—The Harlequin® Reader Service is committed to protecting your privacy. Our Privacy Policy is available online at www.ReaderService.com or upon request from the Harlequin Reader Service.

We make a portion of our mailing list available to reputable third parties that offer products we believe may interest you. If you prefer that we not exchange your name with third parties, or if you wish to clarify or modify your communication preferences, please visit us at www.ReaderService.com/consumerchoice or write to us at Harlequin Reader Service Preference Service, P.O. Box 9062, Buffalo, NY 14269. Include your complete name and address.

LISLPDIR13R